Saved

by a

SEAL

Cat Johnson

ISBN-13:978-1501077289
ISBN-10:1501077287

ACKNOWLEDGMENTS

I could not have created the characters in the Hot SEALs series without having read *No Easy Day* written by Mark Owen with Kevin Maurer. This autobiography of a SEAL provided me with a glance into the minds, attitudes and characters of the men who sign up for this challenging life. It also would not be the story it is without the eagle eyes of my personal military consultants who check for the civilian mistakes I make. That said, any mistakes or liberties taken with the facts are purely my own.

CHAPTER ONE

Zane Alexander watched as his teammate Jon strode across the bar toward him.

"Good. You're here." Jon dumped a binder on the table.

The papers inside were heavy enough to make the beer in Zane's pint slosh when the binder landed.

Zane raised a brow as he picked up his glass. "Whatcha got there, bud?"

"That's the completed business and marketing plan, all put together." Jon pulled out a chair and sat. "Rick and Darci looked it over and then both Ali and I proofread it twice, so it should be ready to present to your father."

Grateful he'd been left out of that incredibly boring stage of this project, Zane eyed the tome. "Nothing else? That's all?"

Frowning, Jon flipped open the front cover of the binder. "I think so. Brody's artwork for the logo is in there, along with a complete company branding section. I also cited and included all the materials I used for research to back up the idea. You know, as proof there's a need for this kind of operation—" Jon glanced up, and then scowled as his shoulders slumped. "You're fucking with me."

"I am." Amused that Jon had finally figured it out, Zane raised his glass in a toast to his gullible friend. Apparently, Jon was a little slow in detecting sarcasm today.

Zane took a swallow of the brew that was already getting warm. He'd arrived early for this meeting with his current teammate and soon-to-be business partner.

Truth be told, he'd needed the drink. Zane had faced the enemy with less trepidation than he felt now on the way to see his father—and the enemy had been carrying automatic weapons with the intent of killing him at the time.

His father utilized weapons that were more subtle than machine guns and explosives, but no less destructive. Zane should know. He'd been dodging his father's verbal shots for as long as he could remember.

He still had yet to figure out how his mother, bless her heart, had survived so long married to his father. By keeping her head down and remaining below the radar, most likely.

Zane had a tendency to get right in his father's face, or he had until that day he announced he was joining the Navy and walked out with nothing but what fit in his bag.

Thank God for the trust fund his maternal grandfather had set up. Zane's father could—and had—cut him off from the family wealth and support, but even he didn't have the power to take away the trust fund in Zane's name or the monthly allowance it yielded him.

Not that Zane's expenses were huge—living in the bachelor barracks when not deployed was cheap—but Zane did like having nice things. Big trucks. Fast cars. Hot women. That all took a good amount of cash. More than he made from his military pay, so the check was surely welcome when it appeared in his account each month.

"Do you want to take a look at what I put together?" Jon looked a little disappointed. Almost crestfallen that Zane hadn't jumped to devour the binder page-by-page.

Even with the kickass winged anchor logo and company name they'd come up with on the front of it, the binder looked too much like the schoolwork he'd always hated.

Zane knew he should review the material before he met with his father later that day, but it could wait. "I will. Later."

Procrastination was one of the many things Zane excelled at. He took another sip of his beer and ignored the book Jon had nudged toward him.

He'd be drinking whisky if he didn't have to get behind the wheel and leave for his drive to the capital region in an hour or so.

When Jon looked ready to crawl out of his skin, Zane decided to relieve his friend's pain. "Look, Jon, I know you and you are incapable of giving less than one hundred percent to anything you do. I trust you that everything I'll need is in that thing, plus some. But the truth is, it doesn't matter what's in your plan. My father is going to give us the money for this company."

Jon pressed his lips together and looked unhappy. "I wish I could be so sure."

"You can be. Trust me. When my father sees I'm willing to leave the Navy for this, he'll jump on investing as much money as we need to start GAPS."

GAPS—Guardian Angel Protection Services—was Jon's brainchild and it was a great idea. A company comprised of a group of men with the best training the Naval Special Warfare Development Group had to offer. As combat-seasoned SEAL operatives, they would be experienced experts-for-hire at a time when precision security was a growing need in so many areas around the globe.

With their friends and former teammates Chris and Rick already out, and with Jon and Zane's current contracts about to expire, they had a four-man team to staff GAPS out of the gate, with the promise of more of their teammates joining them in a few years . . . if they could make a go of it.

Zane traced the tip of one finger over the letters of their tagline printed on the paper slipped beneath the clear plastic front of the binder.

We cover your six when God's too busy.

Was he covering his friend's six now, or leading them all down a path of fruitless hope?

Nothing was certain when it came to his father. Well, nothing except the fact that the one thing George Zane Alexander, Jr. could never get over was his son joining the Navy against his wishes.

And Zane hadn't stopped there. He'd taken it one step further by trying out for the SEALs. Then, as soon as he'd proven himself, he went for DEVGRU's Green Team selection and training—the infamous *Seal Team Six* the media liked to shout about.

Even if those actually in the elite unit didn't like or want the fame the media had thrust upon them after the Bin Laden raid, Zane was indeed among the best of the best, in spite of his old man's wishes. The problem was that once he'd reached the top, there was nowhere left to go to piss off his father.

Zane saw Jon's vision for GAPS as the right opportunity at the right time.

To be able to take their skills and use them as they saw fit *and* be their own bosses was tempting. A dream come true.

Of course, that was only *if* Zane got through this meeting with good old George without taking a swing at the man, which was what had almost happened the last Christmas he'd tried going home to play at being a happy family. You don't talk badly about the troops or make disparaging remarks about the war to a man who had watched friends get blown up. Zane clenched his jaw and pocketed the anger that memory raised.

If nothing else, Zane knew he should see his mother. Thanks to his recent six-month deployment in Afghanistan it had been too long since he'd visited her.

It wasn't her fault the man she'd married had turned out to be a dick. Georgie probably had some charm back in the old days that hid the asshole beneath. Zane had to believe that, or else it meant his mother was an incredibly poor judge of character.

"Where's the waitress?" Jon glanced over his shoulder and then back at Zane. "The one time I really need a beer to calm my nerves, she's nowhere to be found."

"Nerves?" Zane let out a snort. "I've seen you face down the barrel of a gun without blinking an eye."

"True, but dying is easier than failing. At least for me."

Zane knew exactly how important this company was to Jon, and starting it was contingent upon him getting the startup capital out of his bastard father. After that thought Zane needed another beer as much as Jon did.

He pushed his chair back from the table and stood. "I'll go up to the bar and get us a round."

Jon braced his palms against the edge of the table. "No. Sit. I can go."

Zane held up a hand to stop Jon. "Nope. I got it. The waitress is probably ignoring us because of me anyway."

Jon raised his brows high. "What did you do now?"

"I kinda ditched her the other night and went home with someone else." Zane lifted one shoulder in a shrug. "Not my fault. I never promised her anything more than a good time."

"You never do." A smile quirked up one corner of Jon's mouth. "You really shouldn't commit to your fallback lay if there's a chance you're going to take someone else home."

"I didn't expect to. This redhead came in, close to closing time, looking smoking hot and ready for action. What was I supposed to do? You know a new girl will always take precedence over one I've had already."

Drawing in a deep breath, Jon shook his head. "So you keep saying, but I'm perfectly happy with the same girl night after night so . . ."

Zane dismissed that with a sweep of his hand. "You and Ali don't count. You've only been dating for what? A couple of weeks? Less than a month. That's still the honeymoon period when you're just happy to be getting regular sex without having to work for it. You'll move past that stage quickly enough. You'll see."

"Thanks for the prediction and the vote of confidence." Jon rolled his eyes. "And, yeah, you can go up and buy me a draft since you pissed off the waitress. Thanks."

"You got it." Zane pivoted toward the bar. Thankfully, the bartender was male and didn't seem to give a shit who his customers left with at night.

Beer Zane could easily deliver to his friend. A million dollars start-up money contingent upon his father's generosity? That was going to be a little more difficult, but he'd do anything he had to do to get that money. He just hoped it didn't cost him a piece of his soul.

Unfortunately, deals with the devil generally did.

CHAPTER TWO

The drive wasn't incredibly long from base to where Zane had grown up in the outskirts of the Washington D.C. suburbs. The affluent county his family resided in was commutable to the capital, but far enough away to allow for large homes on even larger properties, appealing to the rich and the politically inclined.

Though traffic could easily double the length of the trip, wouldn't you know it, the one time Zane had been hoping for some good traffic delays it was smooth sailing all the way to the parking structure for his father's building.

Zane pulled off his dark sunglasses as he entered the dim lot, easing his convertible to a stop. He reached for the ticket the machine spat out and grabbed it as the mechanical arm rose to allow him access. He cruised up one level and found a nice spacious corner spot to safely park his pride and joy.

Each step brought him closer to the dreaded meeting.

Setting up the meet had been easy. His father's assistant, Amy, had handled it all. Zane hadn't had to even hear the old man's growl on the phone.

As the time ticked on, he found himself hoping that maybe old Georgie had been pulled away for some other business. Then he could hand off Jon's precious binder to Amy and go.

He knew that wouldn't be enough anyway. There were negotiations involved. His future in exchange for his father's investment—God help him.

Zane worked to keep his breathing slow and steady in the elevator ride up to his father's floor. Of course, the man chose an office up high. Better view. More prestige. Whatever. Being closer to heaven wouldn't make George Alexander's soul any less black.

All too soon the brass sign next to the door heralding the company's name faced him. *Alexander Investments*. As he reached for the knob, he couldn't help notice that he'd entered known insurgent dwellings with less trepidation. He wrote that off to the fact he'd been up against his father for many years before the Navy had given him the tools to deal with adversity.

That Zane didn't recognize the first person he encountered, the girl at the front desk, was proof of how long he'd stayed away. Then again, he wouldn't be surprised if there was a revolving door of lower level staff in this company.

"Zane Alexander. I'm here to see my father."

She glanced at the day's schedule, still kept in an old fashioned calendar on the desk rather than the computer. Typical of his father's never changing ways. The girl ran a finger down the list of appointments and finally nodded. He felt a moment of relief that he was actually on the list.

There were layers of personnel to get through before he'd reach the inner sanctum. At least he'd cleared the first one.

"Yes, sir. You can go on back. It's straight and then a right down the hall until—"

He raised one hand to stop her from giving him directions to the office he'd visited with his mother since before he could walk. "I know. Thanks."

Zane made his way through the labyrinth of Alexander Investments, taking note he only recognized two people from among the many new fresh faces he passed.

His father's assistant, Amy, glanced up from her desk as he stepped into her open doorway. Her smile was warm enough to soothe his rattled nerves.

The worst part of the whole situation was that SEALs didn't get rattled. Not in combat. Not when facing death. He'd trained long and hard to ensure that, yet one visit to his father seemed to undo all those years of training.

"Zane. Good to see you." She stood and walked around the desk.

"Good to see you too, Amy. There are so many new faces around here. . ."

"That you're happy to see my *old* one?" She hugged him and then pulled back to shoot him a grin.

He couldn't help but return her smile. "You're not old."

"Well, I'm certainly not young." She laughed. "You look good."

"Thanks." He'd felt good, until this visit. Zane glanced at the closed door behind her. "Is he here?"

"He is, and expecting you."

The binder seemed heavier in his grasp as he felt less prepared for this confrontation than he should. If this had been a mission, he would have devoured and memorized the contents in their entirety.

As it was, he'd barely glanced at the thing. It went against everything he did on a daily basis.

What the hell had gotten into him that he was walking into a situation unprepared? One more look at the door sent his pulse racing and Zane realized his father had gotten to him.

Amy moved back to her desk and hit the intercom button on the phone. "Zane is here to see you."

"Send him back."

Just hearing his father's voice through the speaker upped Zane's stress level. "Thanks, Amy."

He swallowed and moved toward the door. Instead of the weight of the kit that contained his equipment and the tools of his job, today the binder was Zane's only backup.

At the moment he'd give anything for his team to back him, but this was his fight and his alone.

After one bracing breath, he turned the knob and swung the door in. "Father."

"Zane. What brings you here after so long?"

Dig number one, and he'd barely cleared the

door.

"I have an opportunity you might be interested in."

"You mean you need something from me."

Zane noticed with petty satisfaction that his father had put on weight, which only added to the size of his jowls as the corners of his mouth turned down.

He felt his jaw tense and tossed the binder onto the heavy wooden desk before sitting in the leather chair opposite his father. He took his time, forcing himself to move slowly to unnerve the man with his nonchalance.

"Well of course, Father, the proposal would require capital. What investments don't require buy in? Surely none worth anything."

The older man cocked a brow. "Don't try to talk business, boy. It doesn't suit you." He eyed the binder's cover and frowned. "*Guardian Angel Protection Services*. What the hell is that?"

"It's all outlined in there if you'd like to take a look." Zane would rather have his father read Jon's precisely thought out and edited words, than wing this on the fly.

He knew the concept like the back of his hand. Hell, he lived the procedures for his job. But to explain it here and now, out loud and in words good enough to impress his father? No. That would be setting himself up for failure.

After a deep sigh, George flipped open the front cover. Zane knew the first page contained their mission statement. When his father looked as if he'd actually taken the time to read what was written before turning to page two, Zane allowed himself to feel a modicum of encouragement.

In silence, the man flipped through more pages until he finally halted at one.

"*The God Plan*?" George's snowy brows that looked as if they needed a good trim rose high.

Zane leaned over and saw the page header—*Guardian Operational Defense—the GoD Plan.*

Damn, Jon had gotten creative with this shit, and in depth, outlining all the potential services GAPS could provide and even naming them with catchy acronyms.

He probably should have read it all over better before this meeting. Time to tap dance. "The specifics aren't as important as the concept. The point is that too many corporations think they're immune to attack, when in reality no one is. Do you think Maersk ever thought their container ship *Alabama* would be boarded and taken by four untrained Somali's in a skiff and carrying nothing more than a handful of old weapons?"

The reminder erased a bit of the skepticism etched into George's face.

Even if they'd somehow missed the media reports of the event when it had happened back in 2009, most knew Captain Phillips's name, thanks to Hollywood's dramatized version, inaccuracies and all.

Cautiously encouraged, Zane continued. "Same thing for the bank taken over and blown up by a single armed hostage-taker wearing a suicide vest a few weeks ago. Did you see that in the news?"

"I read something about it in the paper."

"Well, I was there. On site. I saw firsthand the police and S.W.A.T. team screw up because those in charge weren't prepared for the situation they had on their hands."

More than just being on site, Zane, Rick, Jon and Chris had been the first men inside the bank after the blast. Before the first responders, even before the dust had settled, because Rick's sister Darci and Jon's girl Ali were inside when it exploded.

"Dad, I stood by and watched that building blow knowing my teammates and I could have prevented it from happening *if* we'd been allowed to."

"And that has to do with this how?" He tipped his head toward the open binder.

"Our hope is that GAPS can prevent attacks from ever happening just by our presence. But even if we're not there prior to an attack, we can be called in and act as a quick reaction force to resolve the situation before it blows up—literally."

George flipped back to the front page where the names of the principal partners were listed, Zane among them. "And what role would you play in this?"

"I'd be part owner as well as an operative."

"An operative?"

"Yes." Zane nodded, happy to answer his father's questions. His interest was a good sign. "I'd work on any jobs we're hired for."

"And the Navy would allow this?"

"They'd have no say in it after I turn in my separation papers."

His father's brows rose again at that revelation, his usual poker face failing him. "So you'd be leaving the military?"

"Yes, sir."

"When?"

"At the end of my current contract. A few months from now." Zane watched for a reaction, but after his initial surprise, his father had tamped down any emotions showing in his expression.

"And why haven't you gone to a bank for a loan?"

"You know I don't have the kind of collateral we'd need for a loan this size. My partners and I have been living off military pay for the last ten plus years."

Zane hoped that zinger struck a cord with the man who had cut him off from the family holdings with one call to the lawyer a decade ago. Though, given he'd come groveling to convince him to fork over a million dollars, he should probably be a little less confrontational.

"Why are the startup costs so high?" Georgie frowned down at one page.

Zane let out a laugh. "Did you see the breakdown of the equipment costs just for each of our basic kits? That's over half a million right there for only four of us."

"And all of this supposedly necessary equipment is currently provided to you by the US Navy?"

Zane didn't consider weapons, ammo or ballistic plates a *supposed necessity*, but he nodded. "Yes, it is."

"So perhaps you should stick with them."

His ace in the hole had been his willingness to quit the Navy. If his father didn't go for that, he had nothing. Heart pounding, Zane tried to play it cool. “I thought you wanted me to quit.”

“Honestly, after all these years, I don’t care what you do.”

“Don’t you?” Zane reeled from his father’s one-eighty, but he’d been too well schooled in hiding his thoughts and emotions to let it show.

He reminded himself that George was a master at playing the game himself. Hiding what he really wanted was what had made Alexander Investments a success. His father was bluffing. If he could do it, so could Zane.

“The truth is, you’re right. I can stay in the Navy for another ten years if I want, and I probably will if you pass on this.” Zane shrugged and let out a laugh. “Headquarters will be relieved actually. Losing me and Jon at the same time, after they’ve invested so much time and money in us, would be a blow to the team.”

“Doubtful. There will always be a fresh crop of idiots lining up. All of them ready and willing to take your place.”

“You’re right about that.” Zane nodded, though the slight had his pulse quickening. He drew in a breath and held it before releasing it to slow his heart rate. “It’ll only take a new enlistee fresh out of boot camp five months to get through BUD/S. *If* he makes it through that, then he’ll have to put in a few years active duty as a SEAL before, *if* he’s selected, he can try out for Green Team. If he makes it, it’s only nine more months of training to get him mission ready. He won’t have my combat experience right off the bat, of course, but hey, he’ll learn. Give him a few more years with DEVGRU, doing what I do and yeah, he'd be my equal."

None of what Zane had said was secret. Any internet search and more than a few autobiographies would reveal the steps necessary to reach the level Zane had.

George scowled at the lecture. "I'm very aware of the time and energy you've devoted simply to spite me."

"Good. Then it wasn't in vain." Zane smiled.

Maybe he had gotten to his father after all. But shit, this meeting had gone downhill fast.

"So you show up wanting something, but what are you willing to give me in return?"

"I'll be getting out of the military, like you've always wanted."

George shrugged. "You'd have to do that eventually anyway. Aren't you getting a little old to be jumping out of planes?"

"No, and when I am I can become an instructor. Hell, I can go to thirty years easily before I retire." He'd do it too, just out of spite.

"Let's say I decide to invest in this GAPS. . ."

Zane tamped down his hope and nodded. "Yes?"

"I'd want fifty-one percent ownership."

"No. Forty percent."

"You want a million dollar investment in nothing more than an idea in a binder for less than controlling interest? Tell me, what would the four of you be bringing to the company in exchange for your sixty percent?"

"Over fifty combined years of training and experience. Some of the best available in the world attained at a cost to the US military that far exceeds your investment. But I can have Jon do the research and come back with an exact figure of our dollar value if you'd like."

"*If* I invest, there'd be another condition, as well." Amazingly, George didn't counter against the sixty-forty split, but moved on.

Zane had no doubt his father would attach something to this deal. The devil always demanded his due. "A condition? Which is?"

"Do you remember Missy Greenwood?"

Zane frowned and pawed through his memories. "The state senator's daughter?"

"That's the one."

"What about her?"

"If I give you the money, you're going to date her. And eventually, ideally, you're going to marry her."

Zane's mouth dropped open, before he managed to close it.

"Problem?" George asked.

"Yes." Zane's voice rose higher. He cleared his throat and continued. "A few."

"Are you already married?"

"No, Father. I'm not." Bad blood or not, he'd have at least informed his father of his marriage. The bastard should realize Zane would never keep something that important from his mother.

George lifted one shoulder in a shrug. "Then I see no problem."

There were too many issues wrong with this scenario to list—chief among them that Zane didn't want to date Missy, or to marry anyone. At least not for a good long while. He liked his bachelor life just the way it was.

Luckily, there were many other complications for him to cite. "For one, what if Missy doesn't want to date me? And even if I do ask her out and she says yes, what's to say she'd marry me?"

"You're a good looking boy. When you're not acting like a child I believe you can be very charming if you'd set your mind to it."

"So I'm supposed to charm a woman I'm not in love with into marrying me? For you."

"That about covers it." George gave a single nod.

Zane was baffled. Of all the things his father could demand he do for this money, this was the dead last thing he would have guessed. "Why?"

"For reasons you don't need to know. You're a soldier. You should be used to following orders without understanding your superiors' reasons behind them."

Typical George, painting everyone the same color with one wide swath of his brush.

"I'm not a soldier. I'm in the Navy. Remember?" Zane ignored George's presumption that he was Zane's superior and corrected the other fallacy.

"That doesn't change anything." George shrugged.

Maybe Georgie was right. It didn't matter. If he was willing to fork over a million dollars in exchange for Zane asking Missy Greenwood out and pretending he liked her, then so be it.

"I want it in writing." If there was one thing Zane had learned in his thirty years on this earth, it was to not trust his father.

The older man nodded. “Consider it done.”

“And you do realize that the investment can’t be contingent upon our actual marriage? Only upon my trying. She could be in love with someone else for all I know. That won’t be my fault if she is. The company still gets the startup money. I want that in the contract.”

His father smiled. “All right, but the effort you expended, should you fail, will have to be evaluated.”

Suspicious at George’s quick agreement, Zane asked, “Who would be that determining entity?”

“A neutral third party. A professional arbitrator, if you’d like.”

“Of my choice?”

“If that will make you feel better, then yes.” George nodded.

Zane didn’t like his father’s compliance. Or his smile. That, above all else, was the most unnerving. George was the kind of man who didn’t smile often and when he did it was usually when he’d just crushed an opponent.

It didn’t matter what George wanted, or what Zane did, there was another element that neither one of them controlled. “I still don’t think Missy will agree.”

“I always knew you were stubborn, but now I’m beginning to believe you’re stupid, as well.”

Zane’s eyes widened at the insult. He’d been away from his father for long enough to forget exactly how abrasive the man could be. “Excuse me?”

“The girl followed you around the country club

like a puppy until you left for your little Navy adventure."

Zane pressed his lips together to hold in a retort to that slight. "Yes, she did. But she was barely a teenager then and I haven't seen her since."

"She's still single. In fact, she's never even had a serious boyfriend, from what I'm told. What does that tell you?"

"That you've become a stalker?"

"It says that she's ripe for the picking. It's perfect timing for an old flame to come back into her life and sweep her off her feet."

This poetic fairytale bullshit coming out of George's mouth was enough to turn Zane's stomach. And that's exactly what it was—bullshit.

"There was never any flame. She's five years younger than me. She was a kid when I knew her. Missy followed me around because there was nothing else to do besides watch our parents get drunk on martinis after playing golf or tennis."

"We'll see." George picked up the phone. "Amy, please write down Missy Greenwood's contact information and give it to Zane. He's on his way out. Thank you."

"I'm leaving?"

"Yes, you are. I have another meeting and you have a date to arrange."

"And you have a contract to have drawn up for us both to sign."

"I'll contact my lawyers. Until it's prepared, your calling on Missy will be a show of good faith on your part."

Zane could be sure of his own good faith. It was

his father's he was skeptical about.

"All right." Zane held up his hand as his father stood. "But if I get recalled, before or even during the date, you do understand I'll have to leave? I'm still bound by my responsibilities."

George lifted one shoulder. "Put in for official leave."

"It doesn't exactly work that way. Leave or not, if they need me, I have to go." Zane was pushing the limits even being here now. If he were recalled, it would be a scramble to get back to base in the allotted time.

"Just do your best, son."

Son. How long had it been since his father had called him that? All the term did was increase Zane's resentment. Apparently, his father only considered him his son when Zane agreed to do what he wanted.

Zane let out a breath. It was no use dwelling on something he couldn't change. He'd gotten what he'd come for—a promise of the money for GAPS. That was all that mattered. "All right. Call me when the contract's ready."

"I'll have a copy messengered to you."

God forbid his father pick up a phone to call his son. Zane resisted the urge to roll his eyes.

"Fine." He turned for the door and left his father's office without a goodbye.

"Here you go." Amy smiled and held out a small piece of paper as he neared her desk.

"Thanks, Amy."

"You're welcome." She smiled wide, and actually looked sincere doing it. "Have a good day."

"Thanks. You too."

How the woman could work with his father for all these years and still be able to smile was beyond him. They must pay her really well. It was the only thing he could figure, but he couldn't devote more than a brief moment pondering Amy's life. He had a girl he hadn't seen in ten years to call and ask out.

Pocketing the paper with Missy's phone number written on it, Zane strode to the door.

Maybe—hopefully—he'd get called in. Somewhere far for a mission that would take a very long time, but not until *after* the contract was signed and the cash deposited into the GAPS bank account, of course.

In the elevator, he typed out a quick text to Jon.

Waiting on the contract but it looks like we got it.

After hitting send, he continued to hold the phone, debating whether or not to call Missy.

The elevator doors slid open and helped make the decision for him as he strode toward where he'd parked the car. Besides, Zane knew Jon and chances were good he would call to talk the moment he read the text. Zane could call Missy later. If he wanted that money, he had to.

He slid into the driver's seat. Next stop, the house he'd grown up in and his mother.

Zane's cell rang barely a minute after he'd hit *send*, and he didn't have to look at the readout on the screen to know who it would be.

True to form, Jon had no patience. His friend was incapable of waiting. It's amazing all the sit-around-and-wait they did on the team hadn't driven the man crazy. That trait was exactly what made Jon so fun to fuck with.

"Hello?" Zane answered the phone with a question in his tone.

"Tell me everything."

"Who is this?"

"It's Jon. You just texted me. Zane, what the hell—"

Zane's chuckle put an end to Jon's rant.

Jon sighed into the phone. "All right. Stop messing around and tell me what happened. Were you serious? There's a contract?"

"Not yet, but there will be."

"So that means he agreed to invest."

"He did."

"The full one million?" Jon's excitement sounded tempered with a good bit of shock.

"Yes, but in exchange for forty-percent of the company. It's a big chunk, but at least it leaves us with controlling interest."

"That's fine. Whatever he wants is fine."

Zane rolled his eyes, glad he'd chosen to come alone. Hell of a negotiator Jon would have been. He would have given the whole damn company away. Then they'd all be working for his father, God help them.

"So how long?" Jon asked.

"I hope soon. With any luck he'll have something for me to sign tomorrow. I'm going to hang here at least for tonight, unless we get called in." It wouldn't kill him to sleep under his father's roof for one night . . . probably.

That would also give him time for the required

show of good faith—the date with Missy.

"So that will be it then? A signed contract and we're good to go?"

"That's it." A signed contract and Zane's bachelorhood, if his father had his way.

Zane kept that little detail to himself. Georgie was his problem to handle, not Jon's.

"Wow. I can't believe it's going so smoothly. Just like you said it would."

"Yup. Smooth sailing." Zane sighed, the note with Missy's phone number on it weighing heavily in his pocket.

CHAPTER THREE

Missy Greenwood surveyed the selection of clothing in the walk-in closet and shook her head. Most of what she owned was totally inappropriate for her trip.

What she needed was a good pair of sturdy boots, cargo pants and about a dozen plain cotton shirts. What she had was a closet full of cocktail dresses and racks filled with designer shoes that hurt after wearing them for an hour.

She turned at the knock on the bedroom door. "Come in."

The door opened and Maria rolled Missy's largest piece of luggage through the door.

"No, Maria. Not the big suitcase. Ask Jorge to take down the smallest carry-on from the attic."

"Just a small one for three months?" A frown creased the maid's brow. "Miss Greenwood, that's not going to be enough."

"It's going to have to be. In fact, if there's a duffle bag or a backpack up there, bring that instead. Do you understand what I mean? A small bag I can carry on my shoulder."

Maria frowned deeper at the request, but nodded. "Yes, Miss. I'll tell Jorge."

"Thank you." Missy wasn't going to count on being somewhere where she could easily roll her Louis Vuitton luggage or find someone to carry it for her. In this case, she had to travel light and simple.

Blending in wouldn't hurt either. Nigeria wasn't Jekyll Island. She wouldn't be rubbing elbows with society folks. The more unobtrusive she appeared, the better. At the girls' school where she'd be volunteering, she'd be among missionaries and teachers, so it would be best to look like one of them rather than as if she'd just stepped out of the country club.

Giving up on the clothes in her closet, she sighed and turned for the door. Packing for this trip would require some shopping first.

She moved to her lingerie drawer and glanced at the contents, realizing she'd need everything right down to new underwear and bras. Where she was headed plain cotton undergarments would be far more practical and more comfortable than her skimpy lace ones would be.

Missy had better go shopping alone too. Her mother would be no help in this situation. Not only did the woman have personal shoppers kissing her feet the moment she walked into any one of the high-end stores in the area, she also didn't approve of this trip. And she sure as hell wouldn't approve of the sturdy, utilitarian clothing Missy planned on buying or the stores she'd likely have to go to find it.

She'd have to sneak out and hit the stores alone.

Her head spun with details. She'd need good comfortable cotton socks, as well. Lots of them, because who knew when or where she'd be able to do laundry? That brought up another point. Should she bring laundry detergent with her? She couldn't imagine there'd be a store near the school to buy any. She wouldn't let herself consider that there might not even be a washing machine.

What she needed was a list.

As Missy turned for the desk to find pen and paper her mother walked in. "Why in the world are both Jorge and Maria ripping apart the attic?"

"They're looking for a bag for me to take to Nigeria."

Martha Vanderbilt Greenwood pressed her lips together until they formed a tight line. Missy resisted the urge to tell her mother that when she held her mouth like that, it created deep and very unattractive wrinkles. Since Missy didn't want to get disowned, she kept her own mouth shut about that.

"I don't know why you insist on going to this place. Can't we just write a nice check to the school instead?"

"No, Mother. They're counting on me being there for the next three months." She knew very well her mother would only be happy when Missy was settled down, married to some *proper* man, popping out heirs and sitting around the country club while some hired woman raised them.

"Schools are always in need of money. I'm certain they'd rather have a donation. That way they can hire a professional teacher. Someone qualified for the job."

The unspoken text in that statement was that her mother felt Missy wasn't qualified. Apparently Missy's double major in English and Education in college and her subsequent Masters degree didn't qualify her to teach English to a group of Nigerian school girls, in her mother's opinion.

"I'm going, Mother. But I agree the school could always use more money, so I'm sure they'll greatly appreciate your generous donation."

Her mother's scowl deepened and Missy flashed back to what this woman used to say to her back when she was a child and would make a face. *Keep that up and it will stay that way.*

Judging by the amount of wrinkles and creases marring her mother's face, giving her the look of being unhappy all the time, it might just be true.

"Anyway, I'm heading to the club for the day. Will you be joining me?" her mother asked.

It was the opportunity Missy needed to get away alone. "No, I can't. I'm running out for a bit."

"Will you be done by dinner?"

"I'm not sure but probably not."

Her mother frowned at that answer. "Where are you going?"

What to say to that? She couldn't utter the word *shopping*. It was practically Martha Greenwood's profession. At the very least, it was her obsession.

"Uh . . ." Missy's cell phone rang and gave her a reprieve, a few moments to breathe and come up with a good excuse to go out alone. She held up one finger to stall her mother. "I have to take this. Hello?"

"Missy? Hi, it's Zane Alexander. I'm not sure if you remember me—"

"Zane, hi. Of course, I remember you." The shock Missy felt was mirrored on her mother's face at the sound of his name.

George Zane Alexander III, her teenage crush. Missy couldn't wrap her head around the fact she was getting a call from him, completely out of the blue, ten years after he'd disappeared so suddenly and completely from her life. What had caused him to pop back into it?

"I'm in town visiting my parents and I was wondering if you wanted to get together." His voice still sent a tremble through her, all these years later.

"Sure. Definitely. When?"

"Are you free today?"

"I am." She eyed her mother, who looked about to burst from listening to only half of the conversation.

"You are?" He sounded surprised to hear that. "Uh, good. Um—I'm trying to think of where we could meet."

"There's a new coffee shop right in the strip of stores on the town square." Killing two birds with one stone, Missy suggested a meeting place that happened to be walking distance to a shopping center where she might be able to find the clothes she needed to buy for her trip.

"All right. That sounds good. Can you meet me at the coffee shop in say half an hour?"

"Half an hour is good. I'll see you there."

"Great. See you there."

She disconnected the call and smiled at her mother. There was no way she would try to tag along now that Missy was meeting Zane. Her family had had their eye on the Alexander heir apparent and his family's fortune right up until Zane had run off to join the Navy.

Missy's teenage heart hadn't gotten over that loss easily. It was a long, painful, angst-filled year after he left before she stopped missing him. Hearing his voice now brought the memories of those days right back, in spite of the time that had passed.

"I'm meeting Zane Alexander for coffee."

"Zane Alexander." The sheer number of unspoken questions swirling through her mother's mind were clearly visible in her expression.

Missy wouldn't have had any answers even if her mother did dare to ask them. She was just as clueless as to what had prompted the call and the invitation to get together after all these years.

No matter what the reason, the timing couldn't have been more perfect. Just when Missy had needed a day away from her mother, Zane had swooped in and given her the perfect excuse.

"Yes. He's in town visiting his parents and wants to get together. I'm not sure if we'll end up having dinner or not, so don't plan on me."

"All right. Please give him our best. And of course, our regards to his family, as well."

"Will do." Missy was about to grab her purse and make a quick exit when she caught a glimpse of her reflection in the mirror.

Her shopping trip had turned into a date, or a least a friendly reunion with the guy who'd taken up every page of her diary during her early teen years. Either way, she wanted to look nice. Right now, she didn't. Not good enough to see, or be seen in town with, Zane Alexander.

"I need to change." Missy sighed and ran her hand through her shoulder-length blond waves, knowing she didn't have time to do anything with her hair.

The unladylike expulsion of breath from her mother told Missy the woman agreed.

"Yes, you do." Fashion guru that she was, her mother strode for the closet while Missy swiped on some blush. She came back carrying a blue wrap-dress and soft leather knee-high, high-heeled boots. "Put this dress on. The color matches your eyes."

"It's cut kind of low in the front for daytime."

Her mother cocked one brow. "And?"

Apparently that was the point. "Okay."

Missy reached for the dress as her mother continued, "Take your beige cashmere coat. It's supposed to get chilly tonight and you might be out late."

Yes, she might. With or without Zane, it would be nice to have the evening to herself. She could take her time shopping for what she needed. Maybe she'd even look for a good traveling bag to buy since Maria hadn't come back from the fourth floor with one.

It was turning out to be a pretty good day after all.

She held the dress up in front of her. It did make her eyes pop, as well as her boobs. Even if they weren't big, Zane would definitely get an eyeful. She wasn't a teenager like she'd been when he'd left. It wouldn't hurt to make sure he noticed the change.

CHAPTER FOUR

Through the dark lenses of his sunglasses, Zane surveyed the passersby streaming past the outdoor café table where he sat. The sidewalk was busy, since it was midday. The temperature was moderate for winter, and the sun was warm enough he'd chosen to sit outside to wait.

Would he recognize Missy? Maybe. Probably. He doubted she'd changed all that much in ten years except for the removal of the braces that had been on her teeth last he'd seen her.

He'd arrived early on purpose. He liked to get the lay of the land before going in. Dating was no different than a mission in that way. He leaned back in the café chair to wait, wondering if having coffee would count as a date in his father's eyes. If he didn't get recalled, he should probably take her to dinner, just to be safe. A little insurance against any sneaky shit George might try.

Glancing at the screen of his cell on the table, he confirmed there were no messages. Not from Missy. Not from the guys either since he had already talked to Jon on the drive over to visit briefly with his mother.

Most importantly, there was no message from command. He might just get this required first date out of the way yet. If Missy wasn't fashionably late, that was.

"Zane." A voice behind him brought his attention around.

He turned to see her smiling and looking the same and yet very different. "Missy. Hello. It's good to see you."

Zane stood and reached out to take her hands in his while he leaned in to kiss her cheek. While doing so he didn't miss the sophistication and maturity a decade had given her. She looked more like her mother than ever, with her large designer sunglasses and expensive cashmere coat.

But the light, cool breeze that turned her cheeks pink and rustled the blond waves brushing her shoulders made her look like the teenager he'd known from the past. So did the genuine warmth in her smile.

She squeezed his hands and Zane felt the chill in her fingers. "We can go inside to sit if you'd like. It's too cool out here for you."

"Actually, if you wouldn't mind, could we get coffee to go?" she asked. "I kind of wanted to take a walk around the shopping center and see what's here."

Zane's brows rose with surprise. This shopping

center? The strip mall filled with discount shops? "Sure. We can definitely grab something to go, if you prefer."

If Zane wasn't very aware that just the clothes on Missy's back cost as much as his military pay for a single pay cycle, Missy's strange request to check out the stores in the strip mall would have him wondering if the Greenwoods were having money problems.

Then again, maybe Missy was more like him than he'd assumed. Maybe she'd traded her access to the family fortune in exchange for freedom too.

Either way, her request upped the interest factor on a date he'd assumed would bore him to death.

He pulled open the door, laying a guiding hand on her shoulder as she walked past him. He could tell from one touch that the coat was cashmere. Authentic designer Burberry and not a knock-off. No doubt about it.

As they joined the tail end of the coffee line behind two other customers, Zane pulled off his sunglasses and took a better look at Missy. "So are you shopping for anything special today?"

She slid off her own glasses and he saw the blue eyes that he remembered being so big they had looked out of place for her face when she'd been a little girl.

"Actually, I am." She drew in a breath like she didn't want to tell him, which made him even more curious to hear. "I need clothes," she finally said.

He grinned. "Don't all women?"

She laughed. "Yes, but not the kind you're envisioning. I'm going to Nigeria to teach English in an all-girls school. I'm thinking my collection of Christian Louboutin shoes might not be the most practical thing to bring with me."

Missy couldn't have said anything that shocked Zane more. "Nigeria? For how long?"

"Three months. I want to be self-sufficient while I'm there, so I don't want to take a lot with me. I'm thinking I need to buy a backpack or some kind of duffle bag with a long strap so I can carry it myself." She cringed. "And when you called it was for us to catch up, not go shopping. I realize that so don't worry. I just thought we could take a walk along the stores and see what's here and then I'll go inside later without you."

He shook his head. "No, it's fine. Actually, I have some experience in some less than friendly environments myself. Maybe I can give you a few pointers on what you'll need."

Less than friendly was an understatement. His last rotation in Afghanistan had his team patrolling in to most of their missions while wearing sixty-pounds of equipment. They'd used the insurgents' own goat paths through the mountains to sneak up on them in their beds in the dead of night. They'd get in and get out, all under cover of darkness, hiking back to base to arrive before the sun rose.

Her eyes, deep blue and guileless, widened. "That would be so great if you had any advice on what I need. I can walk into a boutique and pick out the perfect outfit to wear to almost any occasion my parents require me to be at, but I'm not sure I know how to choose the best hiking shoes and socks."

"And you'll want the right kind of both. Believe

me, your feet will thank you for it."

She still looked hesitant. "Are you sure you don't mind helping me?"

"Not at all. I'll enjoy it." That wasn't even a lie, even though Zane had told many to make women happy.

He moved forward a step toward the coffee counter as the line shortened. This date might turn out to be all right after all. He'd assumed their coffee date would be filled with the latest club gossip or some other crap he had no interest in.

Missy—working in Nigeria and buying hiking boots—that was the last thing he'd ever expected, but it was a pleasant surprise.

Their turn came and he glanced down at her, a good head shorter than him. "What would you like?"

"Large regular coffee, please."

Not the half-caff, low fat, soy, blended, sweetened, overpriced mess he'd expected her to order, but a plain old regular coffee. This girl was full of surprises.

"You got it." He nodded and turned to the barista while reaching for the wallet in his pants. "Make that two, please."

While they waited for the order, she asked, "How are your mom and dad?"

"Good." At least they'd looked good for the short time he'd seen them today, which was the first time in close to a year. He found things remained more peaceful on the family front if he restricted the one-on-one contact. "And yours? Are your mom and the senator well?"

"Very well, thank you. My mother said to send her and my father's regards to you and your parents."

Zane let out a laugh. "That will make my father very happy, I'm sure."

Wasn't getting the senator's notice the whole reason for his father requiring he date Missy? Hell, even marry her—as if that was going to happen.

A crease wrinkled Missy's pretty brow. "You and your father still not exactly seeing eye-to-eye?"

"You could say that, yeah." Zane tossed a twenty on the counter and waited for change from the cashier.

"I was really surprised to hear from you today. In fact, I didn't even know you had my cell phone number." The odd tone in her voice had him glancing at her.

The jig was up. Time to confess . . . at least a small part of the truth. "My father gave it to me. He thought it might be nice if I gave you a call while I was in town visiting."

"Oh." Her brows rose. "I imagine that made calling me the very last thing you wanted to do, because it's what he wanted."

Damn, this girl knew him too well. That was exactly how he'd felt. But not just rebellious, also trapped, like a cornered animal. His father was holding his future in his hands, contingent upon Zane's compliance.

Scary that one visit home could transport him ten years back in his own personal growth. He realized he was still acting like that kid who would always do the exact opposite of what his father wanted.

It was laughable really after all he'd experienced in his life thanks to his chosen career. Things only a handful of other human beings had experienced. Yet, all it took was one visit with his old man to send Zane into a tailspin.

He smiled. "Yes. That's very intuitive of you, and also correct. But only because he still has the power to drive me crazy. Not because I didn't want to catch up with you."

Missy let out a breathy laugh. "Zane, I can assure you, your parents don't hold the exclusive on being able to drive their children crazy. Mine are right up there with yours. Believe me."

Zane reached for the two coffee cups and handed one to her. He tipped his head toward the side counter where the cream and sugar were set out for customers to use and she followed him over.

He put down his cup on the counter and gave his full attention to Missy. "I'm glad I called you . . . even if it did make old Georgie happy."

As she took off her own cup's lid, she glanced up. "Are you really glad?"

"Yes." He imbued the single word with as much sincerity as he was capable of. "You're one of the few people who actually understands what growing up as George Alexander's son meant."

And how much it had messed him up—or drove him to excel and put him where he was today. It all depended how he looked at it. Perhaps Zane owed Georgie a thanks for making him the man he was today.

Her hand paused on the stirrer as she laughed. "Of course, I understand. I've grown up as the daughter of Senator Peter Greenwood. But unlike you, I'm still living at home."

"Proving you're a stronger person than I am." He took the sugar pourer Missy had finished using, surprised once again that she hadn't opted for artificial sweetener like ninety percent of the women he knew would have.

"Me? Strong?" She laughed. "Not really. After all, I am running away to Nigeria just to get some peace."

"I'm not sure that's the place to go if it's peace you're looking for."

Running away for a while was fine, he'd done it himself, but Zane wasn't thrilled with her choice of location.

There was too much unrest, too much going down in that region. Then again, he'd joined the Navy when he'd run away from home. He'd signed up to have people shoot at him for a living, so he really couldn't criticize her choice. He could only hope the missionaries or whoever ran the school she'd be working at had their shit together and were prepared for whatever might happen. Too many times the do-gooders weren't prepared.

"My parents won't be there and that's good enough for me." She replaced the lid on her coffee and looked up. "Ready to shop?"

Zane snapped his own lid into place. "Lead the way."

She took a step toward the exit, before she glanced back over her shoulder. "Prepare yourself. I'm going to need undergarments, as well."

He laughed as he stopped next to her. "I think I'll

survive a trip to the ladies' lingerie department."

"I have no doubt." She looked him up and down before reaching for the door handle.

This was turning out to be a very interesting date, indeed.

CHAPTER FIVE

They hadn't made it more than a few stores down the way, when Zane paused. "Let's go in here first."

"Um, okay." Missy glanced up to see where they were.

Apparently their shopping spree would also include a visit to the pharmacy.

Inside the front door, Zane grabbed a shopping basket and handed it to her. Coffee in one hand, he led the way up and down the aisles, tossing items into the basket she held as they went. Bug spray. Sunscreen. Lip balm, also containing sunscreen.

Finally, they ended in the baby aisle. She frowned as he grabbed for a package of baby wipes.

"What are those for?"

"In case you encounter any sanitation conditions that are less than optimal."

"Oh." She hadn't thought of that.

He tossed in a box of antihistamines. “Take these if you get bit by anything and have a reaction.”

Her eyes widened in horror. “You mean like by a snake?”

His amused grin made him look even more handsome than she’d remembered him being. “I was thinking more of the insect variety. Like bees or spiders.”

That wasn’t much better. “Okay.”

He paused to review the items in the basket. “All right. That’s probably all we need here.”

Zane led the way to the registers in the front of the store. Basket in hand, Missy followed.

While they waited to check out, he glanced down at her. “We should also find you a good hat. You’re fair and it will save your face from burning if you sweat off the sunscreen.”

“Okay.” It was hard to think about sweating when she was wearing a winter coat, but he was right. She was going to Africa.

“That reminds me. Make sure you drink lots of water while you’re there or you’ll dehydrate fast. And if you find yourself not peeing, or if the urine is dark in color, you’re not drinking enough.”

The last thing in the world she’d ever wanted to discuss with Zane Alexander was the color of her pee. Missy cringed. “Okay.”

He dropped his chin to his chest, before looking back up. “I’m sorry. I know this isn’t typical date talk, but it’s important.”

Was this a date? She hadn’t been sure, but apparently he thought it was and she wasn’t going to argue. “It’s okay, Zane. I appreciate all your advice. Really."

He drew in a breath. "Well, as long as we're bordering on the inappropriate, we might as well go get you those new underwear."

"Sure. That would be great." Missy was now regretting that she'd mentioned that back at the coffee shop.

If this was a date, the last thing she wanted was for Zane to help her pick out practical, and likely hideous, cotton granny panties for her trip. Luckily, her turn to check out came and gave her a moment to recover her composure.

Once the transaction was done, she turned to him. "Where to next?"

He took the plastic bag from her hand. "The sporting goods store."

"Okay. Lead the way."

Zane settled his hand on her shoulder. It was only to guide her out the door and in the direction of the store, but the physical contact still had her hyper aware of him. His closeness. His touch. The fact that if he'd touched her like this ten years ago she would have been walking on clouds for a solid week. She was feeling like a teenager as it was.

"I know it's going to sound crazy, but I'm going to suggest you invest a bit of money on some quality underwear." When he saw her brows rise, he laughed. "No, I'm not talking La Perla."

She laughed, not all that surprised Zane knew about high-priced designer ladies' lingerie. He always had been a ladies' man, even as a kid. He'd walk around the country club charming females both young and old. She was sure nothing had changed in adulthood. He still had the good looks and body to turn any woman's head.

Missy was smart enough to know she wasn't the only one to have had a crush on Zane Alexander.

They'd reached the store and he opened the door for her. "I'm hoping they carry UnderArmor."

"Armored underwear? Is that necessary?"

Smiling, he shook his head. "It's a brand most of us wear under our uniforms. Having a good, moisture-wicking first layer that doesn't chafe is a blessing, I promise you. Athletes and the military have similar requirements for performance wear so a sporting goods store should have what we need."

Zane obviously was more than just a pretty face. He knew a lot about a whole lot of things. She knew he'd been in the Navy since he'd left home. She just hadn't considered how many things that might have exposed him to and taught him. Things she should probably know before venturing into unknown territory herself.

Inside the store, Zane surprised her by actually asking for directions to the section they needed. She would have pegged him for the kind of man to wander around for an hour before he'd ask, but no, he'd strode to the front desk the moment they were inside the door.

Now, he stood between a rack of sports bras and one of tank tops "I know this brand is good. I have a couple of shirts made out of it. It's lightweight and breathable." Looking a little lost, even if they had found exactly what he'd asked for, he said, "You'll, uh, have to find your size."

Amused, she watched him avert his eyes rather

than size up her chest. "All righty. Will do."

This wasn't awkward at all after the many nights she'd spent lying in bed and wishing the teenage version of Zane would notice her late-blooming chest. Sure. Missy resisted the urge to groan. She flipped through the sizes and grabbed a bra that would fit her, hoping he didn't see the embarrassing A-cup on the size label.

She located a second one in a different color and said. "Okay, got 'em."

He dipped his head in a nod and moved to another rack. "Next. Underwear."

"Great. And look, they even have thongs." Her cheeks heated as she joked.

Zane laughed. "I'm sorry. I'm sure this has to be the worst date you've ever been on."

There was that word again. *Date*.

She'd dragged him shopping. It was her own fault she was standing with Zane Alexander choosing underwear.

Missy shook her head. "Not at all. Believe me, I've been on some pretty bad dates."

"How about we have a do-over? After we're done getting everything you need, I'll take you to dinner."

Missy couldn't stop the smile that bowed her lips. "I'd like that."

"Great. We'll plan on it then. As long as I don't get called back to base, we're good." He pulled out his cell phone, checked the screen, and shoved it back into his pocket.

Once she could wrestle her mind off exactly how good Zane looked in his khaki pants that hugged his butt just perfectly, she asked, “They can call you back at night?”

He laughed. “Yes. My job isn’t exactly nine-to-five. I’m always on a one-hour recall with the base.”

Her brows rose. “I didn’t realize. Where’s your base?”

“The Virginia Beach area.”

“We’re farther than an hour drive from there. Especially if there’s traffic—”

“It’s fine. I put in for a few days of personal time. My commander knows where I am, so I have a little leeway, but I’ll still have to go immediately if they need me. So far, I’m in the clear.” He shrugged and glanced at the rack of panties. “Anything strike your fancy?”

Picking panties together. This was a hell of a reunion with the guy she’d loved from the moment she’d hit puberty. After this, and the awkward urine discussion in the drugstore, dinner conversation should be a breeze.

“I think these should be good.” Anxious to be done with this portion of the shopping trip, Missy flipped through and selected half a dozen boy short-style underwear in her size.

Glancing at Zane, she noticed him checking his phone again. She took that opportunity to grab a couple of pairs of the thongs, as well. A girl never knew when she might need them.

CHAPTER SIX

"So I was thinking the club for dinner. That all right with you?" Zane glanced at Missy in time to see her cringe. "Or maybe not."

She shot him a sideways look. "It's just that I'm sure my parents will be there. Probably yours too."

That was exactly the point of Zane's suggestion. He wanted his father to get a good look at him with Missy. A show of good faith before they both signed on the dotted line, like his father had suggested in their meeting.

"Is that a problem?" he asked.

"No, it's not a problem for me, if it's not a problem for you."

Zane felt the reluctance radiating off her but in this situation he intended to take her words at face value. No doubt over her lifetime she'd had about as much of her parents sticking their noses in her personal life as he did. Unfortunately, he was beholden to his father at the moment.

"Not a problem for me at all. I'll call and make reservations." For a million dollar investment to make GAPS a reality, he'd put up with having dinner in the fishbowl that was the country club.

"All right." She watched him pull his cell out of his pocket and hit a few buttons. "You know the number?"

He smiled at her as he punched in the phone number he'd memorized so many years ago. "How could I ever forget it? If I wanted to talk to my parents as a child I had to call the club since that's where they usually were. Remember, those were the days before everyone carried cell phones. Though you're young enough, you might not remember that."

An adorable frown creased her brow. "I remember. I'm not that much younger than you."

"Five years," he reminded her as he pressed the phone to his ear.

The five-year age difference when he'd known her before he'd left for college and then the Navy had seemed huge. That was back when she'd been thirteen and he'd been eighteen with a car and an agenda worthy of any guy that age.

Now, the difference was nominal, especially given Missy's level of maturity.

Zane was impressed and more than relieved she hadn't turned out to be the spoiled, immature brat he'd feared she'd become from growing up in this kind of environment.

The sophisticated, smart, independent woman before him was a pleasant surprise indeed. He had asked her out under orders from Georgie, and doing anything to please his father left a bad taste in his mouth, but Zane had to admit that after spending some time with Missy he didn't hate this assignment. Not at all.

After a number of rings, the front desk attendant finally answered, spouting out the country club's name before saying, "How can I help you?"

"I'd like to make a reservation for two for dinner tonight. The name is Zane Alexander."

"Yes, sir. What time?"

He should probably change for dinner. The collared, short-sleeved golf shirt he wore would be appropriate for lunch, but not for dinner at the country club.

Good thing he'd thrown a variety of clothing in the bag in the trunk of his car. It was always best to be prepared. He could change in the men's locker room at the club, but he wasn't sure what Missy wanted to do. She looked great in that dress, but she might want to change before dinner.

"Um, hold on and let me ask." Zane covered the phone and said to Missy, "What time should I make the reservation for? Do you need to go home first?"

She glanced down at the blue dress she wore. "I think I'm good. No?"

"I think you're perfect."

It had taken all his self-control to keep his eyes on Missy's face once she'd taken her coat off. The dress fit her like a glove, accentuating Zane's favorite parts of the female anatomy to perfection.

He pressed the phone back to his ear and said, "I guess six."

They could head over early and have a drink at the bar, before sitting down to eat an early dinner. He was hungry since he'd skipped lunch.

"That's a reservation for two at six o'clock. See you then, Mr. Alexander." The female receptionist confirmed the information.

Being called Mr. Alexander felt strange. He'd been called a variety of things during his last ten years in the Navy, but Mr. Alexander was never one of them. That name was reserved for his father, in Zane's opinion, but he thanked her anyway and then disconnected the call.

He turned to Missy. "We have a little bit of time yet. Is there anything else we need to get while we're out?"

After hitting a bunch of stores, they had enough bags filled with her purchases that it took the both of them to carry it all. She should be covered from head to toe, literally, since they'd picked up everything from a hat to boots, with plenty of items for the parts in between, but she was embarking on a three-month adventure the likes of which he was certain she'd never experienced.

He wanted her to feel prepared, but at the same time, not have so much stuff it would be impossible to transport easily. There were times when, in a strange land, a person needed to be light on their feet. Both for normal travel and for emergencies. He hoped to God Missy never experienced the latter.

"Since we have time, I did want to look at some bags. I don't think there's anything appropriate at the house. You know, something that will fit everything I need, but that I can carry on my own.

I'm not sure where to go to find that here. Maybe back to the sporting goods store?"

Zane smiled as Missy voiced his thoughts almost exactly. "I know right where to go and it won't take us too far out of our way when we head to the club. Want to follow me in your car?"

"Sure."

After a short drive, they reached their destination. Zane pulled into the parking lot first. He cut the engine and got out, leaning against the car as Missy parked in the spot next to him.

He opened her car door for her as she glanced at the building and then at him. "A military supply store?"

"Yes, ma'am. Say what you want about the modern military, but there's one thing that hasn't changed over the years. We end up toting around a whole lot of crap, and that requires some darn good bags to do it. Come on."

Missy laughed. "All right. I've already got military quality underwear. I might as well get the bag to match."

"There's the spirit." He grinned and rested his hand on the small of her back as they walked to the door. He reached to pull the glass door open for her.

Wide eyed, she walked through. "Come here often?"

"Not lately, no. I haven't been around in so long, I'm actually glad it's still here." He led the way down one aisle and to the back wall where the bags were displayed. He paused in front of the selection and glanced down at Missy. "See anything you like?"

"Um, which do you recommend?" She looked understandably overwhelmed.

Zane, on the other hand, was intimately familiar with most of the style bags on display and which bags experience had taught him were the most practical for him. Those, however, might not be the best for Missy. "I'm thinking it will be easier for you to carry two smaller bags than a single big one."

She nodded. "That makes sense."

"When I'm not on a mission, I usually use a three day pack and a helmet bag for normal travel. That's what I've got in the car now for this visit. But instead of a helmet bag with short handles, you might want a bag with a single padded shoulder strap you can wear across the body, like that sling-style messenger bag there." He started looking in earnest at the selection, reaching up to grab a couple of styles so she could see how it felt to carry them. "Good, they have the three day pack in black."

She laughed. "Basic black, so it will match anything?"

"That's a side bonus but actually it's because I don't want you looking like you're associated with the military. It can make you a target overseas, so no camouflage. Okay?" He turned to see her expression of concern. "I'm sure it will be fine, but why take chances, right?"

Missy nodded. "You're right. Thank you."

He'd scared her. Zane could see that. Resting the bags on the floor, he reached out and put a hand on each of her shoulders. "Just be smart. Stick with the others. Don't do anything foolish. Get in, do exactly what you're supposed to do, and then get out. All right?"

Her eyes met and held his. "All right."

Satisfied she was calmer, he nodded and dropped his hold on her. "Try a couple of these and see how they feel. The advanced three day pack is bigger than the regular three day pack, but I'm afraid if you fill it up it will be too heavy for you to manage for any length of time."

Zane was looking around them for something to fill the bag with to simulate the weight of it fully packed when he caught her smile. "What?"

"I like seeing this side of you. The tough take-charge military side."

It was nice that his talking about packs made her happy, but Zane had a feeling she wouldn't like the real military side of him if she could see the reality of what his job entailed. The split second decisions he made on a daily basis that resulted in life or death for the targets. The emotional detachment that came from his years with the teams. The addiction to action that rode him as hard as any drug.

Those things wouldn't have her smiling. Wouldn't have put the warmth in her gaze that oozed with a hero worship so much like the one he'd seen in the face of the little girl who used to follow him around.

He turned his focus back to the task at hand. "Come here. Give this bag a try."

"Yes, sir." She delivered a totally incorrect but enthusiastic salute and then slipped the messenger bag he held out over her head.

Meanwhile he couldn't help but think she was

too young, too innocent, too damn blond and American-looking to be traipsing around Nigeria unprotected.

If he told her that, if he expressed his concern, would she change her mind?

Probably. She'd do anything he wanted back in the old days. Run to the snack bar to get him a soda. Wash his first car while he'd lounged in a chair by the pool and ogled all the young trophy wives in their bikinis. He'd been sixteen and obnoxious that year, taking shameful advantage of her. Now, it was real concern for her well being that motivated him to try and influence her.

Still, did he have the right to change her plans? To prevent her from spreading her wings. He'd done the same when he'd left home to join the Navy and then the SEALs.

How could he begrudge her this if it was what she truly wanted to do?

He couldn't, but he could make sure she was as safe as possible. "When you're done with that, I'd like to go take a look at the knives."

"Sure."

"You flying commercial?" he asked.

"Yes."

"Will you be checking the big bag?"

"Yes."

"Good. Then it shouldn't be a problem if you've got the knife packed in the checked baggage."

Missy lifted her brows high. "The knife is for me? I thought you wanted to look for you."

"No. I've got plenty of my own. This one is for you."

Her mouth fell open, before she asked, “Why?”

To protect herself from the many horrors that could befall a young woman in a foreign country, that’s why. What Zane thought and what he said were two very different things. “A good knife has too many uses to mention. And better to have and not need, than to need and not have, right?”

“Okay. I trust you.”

She trusted him, and he had called and asked her out so his father would give him money. That made Zane feel like a complete piece of crap.

Missy slung the messenger bag over her shoulder and posed for him. “I think I like this one. It’s actually kind of cute.”

The girl in the Burberry cashmere coat thought a military surplus canvas bag was cute. The ridiculousness of the situation had him laughing in spite of his guilt.

“No, you’re the one who’s cute.” He watched as she met his gaze and then shyly dropped her eyes away from his.

The situation with his father and the reason for this date was too fucked up for him to be able to handle how intense things were starting to feel with Missy.

He’d done some less than honorable things in his personal life, but he was most comfortable being upfront with the women he spent time with. Sex with no strings or a one-night stand presented no moral dilemma for him as long as his female counterpart knew what she was getting into up front. Before the clothes came off, he liked to set things straight.

It all boiled down to expectations. If she expected more than he was willing to give, then that was the time for Zane to walk away. He wasn't out to cause anyone heartbreak. But this situation with Missy, forced upon him by his father, went against the very philosophy that Zane tried to live by—open honesty.

Maybe he'd be better off telling her the complete truth, but that could hurt her worse than simply keeping the charade to himself. It would be so much easier for both of them to just let her go off to Nigeria for three months never knowing.

Zane liked his love life simple—catch and release, and then move on. The problem was, Missy wasn't anything like his usual prey.

Damn his father to hell for choosing this particular girl as the condition for the investment.

While Zane was at it, he cursed Jon for coming up with the idea for GAPS that had put him in this position in the first place.

He resented Missy too for being so damn sweet that she'd made him like her. Made him wish he were the kind of man who could be happy having a girlfriend or a wife, instead of the man he was. One who could only be happy with the next new conquest.

That brought him full circle, back to hating his father for demanding the one thing Zane couldn't give—commitment at the expense of his freedom.

He reached out and took the messenger bag from Missy. "Choose which size pack you want and then we can head to the knife counter."

CHAPTER SEVEN

Missy wove her way through the sprawling acres of manicured grass along the driveway that led to the clubhouse. She crept along in her car at a snail's pace in reverence to the golfers who sometimes crossed the driveway.

She'd grown up at this club, spending every day during the summer here. She'd eaten meals, learned to swim, golf and play tennis here. Celebrated birthdays and holidays, had made friends and had lost them, all while here.

And she'd fallen in love here—or at least she thought she had.

As a teenager it had been easy to believe she'd die of a broken heart if Zane Alexander didn't fall as deeply in love with her as she was with him. But she hadn't died in spite of the fact it had felt as if she would when he'd left, first for college, and then for the Navy.

She glanced in the rearview mirror and saw him, convertible top down, sunglasses on, his light brown hair windblown. A foursome of ladies standing at the tee all turned in unison like a team of synchronized swimmers to watch Zane drive by. She was sure it would be the same in the dining room. It always had been, but tonight Missy would be the one who'd be sitting opposite him.

This time yesterday, if someone had told her she'd be having dinner with Zane after spending the afternoon shopping with him she would have told them they were crazy. It was hard to believe even now, but the proof was in the sports car creeping slowly along behind her.

Missy pulled up in front of the massive clubhouse and cut the engine, leaving the keys in the ignition for the valet.

He opened the car door for her. "Good evening, Miss Greenwood. Should I keep the car in the courtyard or will you be staying awhile?"

"I'm having dinner."

"Very good." He nodded and slid behind the wheel. He pulled away to park the car in the lot as she moved to the wide set of front steps to wait for Zane.

The impressive stone building had been built in the late eighteen hundreds. It always gave Missy the feeling of stepping back in time when she walked through the front doors. Aside from the modern cars outside and the sign requesting cell phones be put on silent just inside the massive front doors, she supposed it hadn't changed all that much over the centuries.

Neither had the members. There would always be those families with old money who looked down upon those with new money. Men—white, straight, and Protestant—still dominated the club's board, while their wives, also of the same demographic, gossiped behind each other's backs while smiling to one another's faces.

This place was truly stuck in the past and, sadly, Missy feared it wasn't about to change soon. That was one reason why she'd been so surprised when Zane had suggested they eat here. Nothing, including the menu, had changed over the decade since he'd abandoned this life.

Speaking of Zane, she realized he hadn't pulled up behind her. Instead, he'd parked his car himself in the lot. She saw him now, jogging toward her with a bag not much different from the one she'd purchased in his hand.

She smiled as he neared. "Don't trust the valet to drive your baby?"

"I feel more comfortable having control of my keys."

That was interesting. The club grounds had always been secure. There was no danger of theft here. "Really?"

Zane hesitated and then drew in a breath. "I've got a weapon locked in the glove box."

"Oh." Her brows rose at that revelation. It always had been hard for her to reconcile the memory of the rarely serious boy she'd known growing up with the hardcore image of a man who'd made the military his career.

He took her by the elbow, steering her toward

the door. As they walked, he leaned low and close to her ear. “Don’t worry, I won’t have anything dangerous on me for dinner. At least, not a weapon.”

The warmth of his words against her ear sent a shiver traveling down her spine. She glanced sideways and saw his grin. “That’s good to hear. I wouldn’t want something to go off during dinner and give any of the older members a heart attack.

He grinned wider. “Would never happen. I always have complete control.”

That was too bad. As he put his bag down on the bench inside the front hallway and helped Missy off with her coat, she decided she wouldn’t mind seeing Zane lose a bit of that control with her.

With a wink and a smile, Zane handed her coat off to the woman manning the coatroom and Missy realized something. Just like in the old days, Zane still flirted with every female he came in contact with. Young and old alike. With both strangers and old friends.

His joking with her when they’d first walked in, his double entendre about his control of his loaded weapon, was likely as far as things would ever go between them. He’d called her because his father had told him to.

That thought was like a bucket of cold water thrown over her good spirits in spite of the warmth of his hand against the small of her back as he steered her into the lobby.

“I have to run down to the men’s locker room to change. Do you want to wait for me here in the lobby or in the bar?”

"In the bar." There had been no need to think about her answer. Right about now, Missy needed a drink.

"All right. I won't be long." After shooting her a smile the likes of which she was sure had charmed females around the globe, Zane headed toward the stairs leading down to the locker rooms.

Turning, Missy caught sight of two waitresses whispering as they watched him walk away. With a huff, she strode past them, making a beeline for the bar. Getting through this evening was going to require a nice big drink. Or two. Maybe then she wouldn't care anymore.

She'd already put a bit of a dent in the martini in front of her by the time Zane reappeared. He eyed her glass and then her as he lifted one brow. "I remember a day when you used to sit at this bar and drink Shirley Temples. Extra cherries."

"I'm surprised you remember. That was a long time ago." That he remembered such a small detail from so many years ago only seemed to make her angry.

It wasn't her imagination that they'd been close, and yet he hadn't bothered to contact her in the past ten years.

"I have a good memory." He smiled.

"Apparently."

Zane turned as the bartender approached them. "Whatever light beer you've got is fine."

"Yes, sir."

"Light beer?" she asked.

"Yes, ma'am. Have to watch my figure." He grinned and accepted the bottle, but pushed back the empty glass the bartender had placed in front of him.

She cocked a brow. "I pegged you for a scotch man like your father."

"That's reason enough to order a beer, right there." He raised the bottle to her in a toast and then pressed it to his lips.

"Still stubborn, I see."

"Until the day I die. Enough about me. When do you leave for your trip?"

"In five days. Not that I'm counting, or anything."

He barked out a laugh. "Of course you're not. Just like I didn't count down the hours until I left for college or for boot camp."

She had counted down the hours until he'd left too, but for a different reason.

"What's wrong?" Zane's hand covered hers.

Missy glanced up. "What makes you think anything's wrong?"

"That big sigh you just let out, for one."

Maybe it was the alcohol making her bold, but she decided to tell him exactly what was wrong. "I just would have thought that at least once over the past ten years I would have seen you. Christmas. Thanksgiving. The club golf tournament. I don't know. Some time."

"I'm away a lot. I spent last Thanksgiving and Christmas in Jalalabad. And when I am stateside, I guess I do avoid coming home. Georgie and I don't see eye-to-eye on most things. Hell. On anything, really."

"Yet when he suggested you call me, you did."

"And I'm glad I did." He squeezed her fingers.

She wasn't going to let him off that easily. "You know, there are other people here besides your father. People who miss you. Like your mother."

And Missy too, but she left that part unspoken.

He dropped his chin to his chest. When he brought his head back up, his expression made him look sincerely contrite. "I know and I'm going to try to be better about keeping in touch from now on."

"That's good. I'm sure that will make your mother happy." It would make Missy happy too, but she wasn't about to say that out loud either.

In the months since she'd planned her trip to Nigeria, this was the first time she let herself see past that time, to look forward to returning. It was foolish of her. This was Zane Alexander, the boy who'd been a Casanova since he hit puberty.

People changed. Had Zane?

He tugged on her hand, making her turn fully to face him. "I want you to promise me something."

Her mouth went dry beneath the intensity of his stare. "Okay."

"Be careful over there."

"Everyone said the area where the school is located is perfectly safe. Are you worried about me?" She smiled at the idea he might be.

"Nowhere is perfectly safe. Trust me on that. And yes, I am worried about you."

Maybe she should have gone to Nigeria when she'd been a teenager. If she had known it would garner this much attention from Zane, she might have seriously considered it.

Keeping her pinned beneath his green-eyed gaze,

he reached out and captured her other hand, as well. "Melissa. Promise me."

Hearing her given name from his lips rather than the childish nickname she'd never been able to shake, she found it hard to breathe. Somehow she managed to respond. "I promise."

He dipped his head in a single nod and then dropped his hold on her. "It's after six. We should go sit."

"Okay." Still unsteady just from his touch, she reached for her drink and tried not to spill it as she slipped off the bar stool and followed Zane toward the dining room.

CHAPTER EIGHT

"Look. Your parents are here." After surveying the seated diners in the room, Zane glanced at Missy.

He saw her cringe at his observation before she said, "Yes, they are."

He paused in the doorway rather than go to the maître de stand for their table assignment. "We should say hello before we sit."

"If you insist." She glanced around the dining room and, cocking a brow, sent him a sly sideways glance. "Oh, look. Your parents are here, as well. We'll have to go say hello to them next."

He couldn't help but smile. He liked how this new adult version of Missy gave as good as she got. They certainly were kindred spirits.

It took his hand on her lower back and a gentle nudge to spur Missy into motion. He could have sworn she dragged her feet as they made their way to her parents' table.

"Mrs. Greenwood, you look more beautiful every time I see you." Zane leaned down and kissed Missy's mother on both cheeks before he straightened up and extended his arm to shake her father's hand. "Senator Greenwood, sir. You're looking well. How have you both been?"

The older man pumped Zane's hand enthusiastically. "Good. Good. And how are you, son?"

"I'm very well, thank you."

"It's such a pleasant surprise to have you visiting." Mrs. Greenwood smiled sweetly.

Parents always had loved him. Parents other than his own father, that was.

"I know. I don't visit nearly enough. But maybe that will change in the future." Zane shot Missy a meaningful look. He left his hand resting on her lower back, knowing without a shadow of a doubt that his father would see the deliberate move from across the dining room.

"Oh?" Mrs. Greenwood raised her perfectly shaped brows high. "And why is that?"

"I'm thinking of rejoining the civilian ranks."

Missy frowned up at him. "Really? You didn't mention that today."

Zane lifted one shoulder. "We were having too much fun. It didn't come up. My current contract has a few months yet so it wouldn't be until later this year, anyway. I guess about the time you're getting back from Nigeria, I'll be getting out of the Navy."

One blond curl hung over Missy's eye. He

reached up and brushed it to the side as her gaze met his. He glanced at her parents and saw the interested looks he and Missy were getting from them. No doubt his own parents wore similar expressions. Maybe it was time to go spread the love around.

"I suppose we should say hello to my mother and father and then sit down for dinner. I've kept Missy busy all afternoon and haven't fed her a thing aside from a cup of coffee and that drink in her hand." Zane sent his most charming smile to Mrs. Greenwood.

She allowed him to kiss her one more time on the cheek as she said, "Of course. Sit. It was good seeing you."

"You as well, ma'am." Zane turned from Missy's mother to her father. "Enjoy your dinner, sir."

"You too. Good to talk to you, son. Don't be a stranger."

"I won't." After another hearty handshake from Senator Greenwood, Zane and Missy were finally making their way across the dining room.

"Now it's my turn." Missy said it low enough that only he could hear, before she stepped forward with both hands extended to his parents. "Mrs. Alexander. Lovely to see you."

"Missy, darling. What a surprise seeing you here with Zane."

"We're having dinner. Didn't he tell you?"

"No, he didn't, but it's wonderful seeing you two are catching up."

"It is nice to catch up after so many years." She

shot him a glance and he heard the remonstration in her tone.

It had been too many years since he'd seen or talked to her and Missy wasn't letting him get away with it. This new strong side was one of the traits he was finding he liked best about her.

Missy moved to his father and kissed his cheek. "Mr. Alexander, I heard you bested my father on the course last weekend. He might never recover."

"Eh, he'll get over it." Old Georgie treated Missy to such a genuine smile that it took Zane aback. "Besides, he's got a few other things on his mind with the campaign."

"That he does, but shh. Remember, he hasn't made the official announcement yet."

George nodded. "Right. Well I'll be the first one to back him when he does."

"And I know he appreciates your support. But I should let you two get back to your dinner. We're interrupting."

His mother waved away Missy's concern. "Not at all. We haven't even ordered yet. You should join us."

Missy glanced back at Zane with a sly expression. "Zane, did you want to join your parents for dinner? I know you don't have the pleasure of seeing them as often as you'd like."

The little minx knew exactly how he felt about spending time with his father. She was getting back at him for dragging her over to see her parents. He smiled. "As lovely as that would be, I'm going to be selfish. Mother, Father, with all due respect, I want Missy's undivided attention this evening. Did you know she's leaving soon for three months in Africa where she'll be teaching at a school?"

"No. I didn't know." His mother frowned and turned to his father. "George, did you know that?"

"No, I didn't." Georgie frowned and shot Zane a look filled with suspicion. As if he was lying to get out of their deal.

"I think my parents keep hoping I'll change my mind about going. I guess they think if they don't tell anyone, I'll back out."

Zane let out a snort. "I can't blame them there."

"Zane, I want to go."

"I know you do, but that means we don't have much time to spend together before you do, which is why we'll respectfully take our leave now. If you'll excuse us, the maître de should have our table waiting."

His mother, sweet as always, reached out to squeeze his hand. "Of course. You two go and enjoy your evening. We understand. It was so nice talking with you, Missy."

"You too, Mrs. Alexander. Mr. Alexander." She smiled, charming even a hard man like his father.

It was obvious Missy had been born into this life. She was the quintessential politician's daughter. Good at small talk. Quick to smile. Always knowing the right thing to do and say to everyone. She was pretty much the polar opposite of Zane.

She'd stuck it out in this world. He had to think it took more strength for her to stay than it had for him to leave.

"Zane, will you be staying at the house tonight." Georgie eyed him before he could get away.

"Yes, sir. Unless I get called back to base."

"Then I expect we'll talk later back at the house." The man's tone left no doubt that they would.

"I expect we will. Mother, I'll see you later." Zane forced a smile and, with a hand on Missy's back, guided her away from the table. He leaned toward her when they were out of earshot. "Did you enjoy that?"

"Enjoy what?" Her voice lilted with laughter.

"Torturing me."

"Oh, come now. It wasn't that bad. Your mother is a darling."

"Yes, my mother is."

His mother wasn't the issue. It was the accusation in his father's eyes and the tone of his words that had pushed Zane's blood pressure higher. When he pushed the simmering anger aside, there was something else that had been revealed during the brief conversation with his parents that continued to nag at his brain.

He waited until the maître de had shown them to their table and they were alone before he asked, "What campaign is your father about to announce?"

When Missy glanced around them and then leaned forward before she answered, Zane had to assume this wasn't simply about reelection for his current senatorial seat.

"Only a handful of people know. . ." She paused.

Zane lifted his brow. "Missy, do you know what level of clearance I have? Believe me, you can trust me to keep a secret."

"Of course, I trust you." She leaned in even

closer. "He's hoping to get the nomination at the Republican convention. He's making a bid for president."

Senator Greenwood—running for President of the United States. Of course George Alexander would want to ride the coattails of the politician who could become the most powerful man in the free world. It all made sense now why his father was so interested in joining the Alexanders and the Greenwoods with the bonds of matrimony.

"Zane?"

He'd gone quiet, lost in his own thoughts, and Missy had noticed. He smiled and glanced at the stage where a piano player had started playing background music. "Since when do they have live music during dinner? That's new."

"No, it's not new at all. It started about the time you were in college but you always snuck out by the time the music started." She smiled.

"My loss." He stood and extended his hand to her. "Dance?"

After a look of surprise, she placed her hand in his. "I'd love to."

The feel of having a woman in his arms wasn't unfamiliar to Zane, but that they were on the dance floor and fully dressed at the time certainly was. So was the fact that Missy was a friend. He hadn't realized how much of one until today.

Way back when, she'd been a tag-a-long. Her one and only sibling, a brother, was much older. He'd married and had moved away twenty years ago, so Zane always figured he'd been a substitute brother for a girl who was being raised more like an only child.

Today had shown him they really did have a shared past. He knew her as well as she knew him, then and surprisingly now too. Deep down he was still that same rebellious son quick to want to do the opposite of his father's wishes . . . except for asking Missy out. But Zane had done that not for Georgie, but for Jon. And for Rick and Chris and GAPS.

As Zane steered Missy in slow motion around the dance floor, he appreciated the feel of her beneath his hands. Her warmth. Her curves. Complying with his father's wishes aside, this had to be the easiest assignment he'd had in a long time. He was having no problem taking one for the team.

In her sexy as sin high-heeled boots, which he didn't dare think about too hard while pressed this closely to her, she came up to just above his chin. He detected a fresh, clean aroma. Apples maybe? He leaned lower, resting his cheek against her hair as he breathed in the scent of her.

She leaned into him, lost in the moment, the music, and possibly the martini she'd downed fast enough that it had probably gone to her head.

Not so for Zane. He'd been sipping his one beer, mainly in case he got called in and needed to drive back to base tonight. Of course, there was one other consideration. Too much alcohol made a man do foolish things, such as forget himself. Forget that he shouldn't be taking advantage of the sweet young thing he'd watch grow from a child in pigtails, to a teen in braces, to the woman in his arms who he wasn't going to allow himself to think of as a woman.

If this were any other female and this any other situation he'd be buying her another drink or two and booking a room at a hotel. But this was good old Missy. This was also presidential candidate Greenwood's daughter who Georgie had his eye on to expand the Alexander dynasty.

Zane didn't need any more reasons than that to put Missy firmly in the hands-off category, though doing so would be far easier if his hands weren't currently on her.

His palm braced low on her back, steering her movements, but more keeping her close. His other hand held hers. It felt small and delicate in his, reminding him that this girl wasn't nearly equipped to be alone in Nigeria. She'd spent her life living amid the dangers of the rich and powerful, but that wasn't any kind of training for what she could face on the other side of the world if things went bad.

His protective side was kicking in hard. Considering he didn't have anyone of his own to worry about, at least no one who belonged to him, this was a new and unpleasant feeling. One he had every intention of tamping down and ignoring.

Yes, he was prepared to kill or die in the course of his job on any given day, but that was simply cold hard reality. His career. His life.

This, with Missy, felt more personal. At the moment, with her pressed against him, he couldn't seem to dig down deep enough to find that efficient impersonal machine he'd become from a decade of doing what he did. Instead, he felt warm, soft, human. He didn't like it.

The song ended and another began. Missy lifted

her head from his chest and looked up at him with heavily lidded eyes. Eyes he needed to steer clear of if he was going to keep his head on straight.

Time to get this date back on track. The track Zane had decided it should be on. They'd eat. He'd send her home, with her parents if she couldn't drive, then he'd go back to the house and deal with his father. That would help Zane get his damn act together.

"We should sit back down and order dinner." Zane needed to get some food in Missy's stomach. Make sure she was good and sober. Maybe then she'd look less tempting, because if she sent one more look in his direction like that last one, he wasn't sure he'd be able to resist her.

CHAPTER NINE

Missy sighed as Zane asked her the same question for the second time in less than ten minutes. "I swear I can drive."

"Are you sure?" He eyed her with concern as they stood outside beneath the electric glow of the exterior lights in front of the clubhouse.

"Yes, I'm sure."

Zane drew in a deep breath, and her gaze dropped to watch his chest rise and fall beneath the crisp, cotton button-down shirt he'd changed into for dinner. He shook his head. "I'm not. I wish you would have gone home with your parents and left your car here."

She hadn't wanted to go home with her parents and leave her car there because that would have meant she was also leaving Zane there, and she wasn't quite ready for this night to end.

Two martinis over the course of more than two

hours and a huge meal—she should be able to drive the couple of miles to her house. But that was the last thing she wanted to do with her insides feeling all warm and squishy from the alcohol and Zane's proximity.

"If you're that concerned, perhaps you should drive me home." Missy rested her hands on his chest. Damn. She could feel how big and solid his muscles were clear through the shirt.

He dropped his gaze to where her palms pressed against him, his nostrils flaring as he drew in a deep breath. He nodded. "That's exactly what I'm going to have to do."

He didn't sound very enthusiastic. She drew her brows low in a frown. "Is it a problem?"

Zane let out a laugh and shook his head. "It shouldn't be a problem, no."

He'd said the words as if he hadn't meant them. "Zane, if you have somewhere you need to be—"

"No, I don't have anywhere I need to be. Is your car all locked up?" He glanced at her vehicle.

They'd stayed so long the valet had left for the night, but he'd parked her car close to the clubhouse and had brought the keys in to her in the dining room.

Missy aimed her keys at the car and clicked. The vehicle's lights flashed and the horn let out a single honk, proving the doors were locked. "Yes."

"Then come on."

She didn't like this change in him. He'd been attentive all night. His eyes had barely left her. His attention had never wavered. Now, he was treating her like she was thirteen again and he'd gotten stuck driving her home. That had actually happened once, and she'd felt the same way as she did now. Like she was a burden to Zane.

"No. I can drive myself—"

"Dammit, Missy. Stop. I'm driving you." To insure that, Zane reached out and snatched the keys she still held in her hand.

"But you don't have to."

"But I want to." He smirked down at her as he steered her toward the side lot where he'd parked his car. "Button up your coat."

"I'm fine." Missy frowned as Zane began to remind her of her mother and her obsession with her wearing a winter coat in case it got cold.

He paused next to the sexy sports car that was so befitting the youthful playboy he'd been when he'd been a daily fixture in her life. "You're fine now. You're going to get cold in a minute. I only drive my car with the top down, unless I'm out and get caught in a rainstorm."

There was a storm, all right, but it was her roiling emotions, not the clear night with the stars twinkling above them as he turned to yank the sides of her coat together. He buttoned the two middle buttons as she stood and waited.

A moonlit drive with Zane was her teenaged self's dream come true, and now that it was happening he was buttoning up her coat like she was a toddler. When he reached the top button she frowned deeper. "Zane. Stop."

He leaned down. "Let me take care of you while I can, please. Soon you'll be on the other side of the world."

"With a big scary knife to protect myself with, thanks to you." At her comment, the corner of his mouth tipped up with the hint of a smile.

"Not as big as I would have liked it to be, and I'd be happier if it was in my hand while I protected you, rather than in yours." He reached down and laced his fingers through hers.

This man with his constantly changing disposition toward her was enough to give Missy whiplash. She could chair a not-for-profit board meeting, run a million dollar fundraiser, and play hostess at a party with guests that included the leaders of the free world, all with confidence, but with Zane she had no clue where she stood.

"Ready to go?" he asked.

"No." She wasn't ready yet. In five minutes they'd be at her house and he'd be saying goodnight and driving away. Then who knew when she'd see him again.

He raised one sandy brow. "No?"

She stifled a sigh. "Just kidding. We can go."

"All right." He nodded and walked around to the passenger side to open the door for her.

Reluctantly, she followed. She'd be pouting like a child soon if she didn't watch it.

A vicious circle, this thing with Zane. It was like she was living in two worlds simultaneously. That of a teenaged girl and that of an adult woman. When he treated her like a child, she started acting like one.

Then there were times when he touched her like he wanted more, and that one touch was enough to have her insides turn molten. But the moment passed and then he acted like it had never happened.

Zane settled her in the seat, and even stretched out the seatbelt and handed it to her before he strode around the car and got into the driver's side.

He was just putting the roof down, since he'd had it up while they'd been inside, when he glanced at her. "What's wrong?"

"What makes you think something's wrong?"

"Oh, I don't know. Maybe that you're frowning so hard you're going to get wrinkles if you don't stop." Leaning closer, Zane reached out and ran one finger between her brows.

There he went again. Confusing her with his little touches.

"Remember that summer you were a junior in college?"

"I guess."

"You were dating one of the waitresses." Missy used the word dating as a euphemism for what Zane had really been doing with the girl.

He smiled. "Yeah, I remember now."

"I saw you getting into your car with her one night. My mother had asked me to run out to our car to get her sweater because the A/C in the dining room was so cold and we were sitting right under the vent. Anyway, sitting here in the car with you . . . it just reminded me of that time."

Except for the fact Zane hadn't been able to keep his hands off the waitress. He'd been pawing at her during the walk to the car, and hadn't stopped once they'd sat inside. Missy was sure they didn't make it much farther than the driveway that led to the stables before he'd pulled off the road to have sex with her. Yet with Missy, he was more concerned with making sure her coat was buttoned up tight and her seatbelt fastened.

"I'd completely forgotten about her. Funny, I can't even remember her name." Zane shrugged, and slid the key into the ignition as he glanced at Missy. "Ready to go?"

"Yes." She was ready to be away from the scene of that memory. Maybe then she'd stop comparing the way he'd been with the waitress, compared to the way he was with her now.

Though maybe the glaring difference in the way he treated her was exactly the point. He didn't remember the name of the waitress he'd spent a summer pawing, but he'd remembered Missy had liked extra cherries in her Shirley Temples as a child.

Sadly, cherries weren't going to quench this adult thirst. Only a taste of Zane would do that.

The trip took barely a few minutes and before she knew it, they were driving through the gates at the end of the driveway of her house. Soon, Zane was pulling up right to her parents' front door.

"So, you're going to sleep at your parents' house tonight?" she asked.

"Yes, as long as I—"

"Don't get called back to base." She finished the mantra she'd been hearing all day.

It was strange, this new responsible Zane. A big change from the boy she'd known who'd been late for everything, if he bothered to show up at all.

He smiled and nodded. "Exactly. But if I don't get called in, do you want to do something tomorrow?"

Another one-eighty from Zane had her head spinning. "Sure."

"All right. I'll call you in the morning and we'll decide what you want to do."

"Okay." Missy hesitated, waiting.

When she realized sitting there silently hoping he'd kiss her good night was ridiculous, she reached down to unlatch her seat belt. After she did, Zane covered her hand with his. He leaned in and her heart stopped, until he pressed his lips to her cheek.

A kiss on the cheek like one gave a child. She sat perfectly still as her disappointment changed to something closer to anger.

He didn't pull back after the chaste kiss. He hovered so close it had Missy's pulse pounding. She turned her head to look at him, to try and see his expression through the darkness lit by only the lights on either side of the front door. It was the slightest movement, but it put his mouth closer to hers, which is when he took advantage of the proximity and his lips covered hers.

She drew in a sharp breath at the unexpected contact, which parted her lips ever so slightly beneath his. He responded by angling his mouth over hers and tangling his fingers in her hair to cup the back of her head.

Zane drew in a deep breath and then pulled back. His gaze met hers from just inches away, before he turned away and opened his door.

Before she knew what was happening, he'd run around the hood of the car and was opening her door for her. Stunned and honestly feeling a little wobbly, she took the hand he offered her and stood.

He dropped his hold on her hand the moment she was out of the car. "Good night."

She listened, but his words had been devoid of emotion and held no clues to what he was feeling.

"Good night, and thank you for everything today."

Zane dipped his head. "You're welcome. I'm sorry I didn't think to get the bags out of your car so you'd have everything you bought with you tonight. You know, in case you wanted to start to pack."

Packing was the last thing on her mind as her head spun with a kaleidoscope of thoughts and emotions. "That's okay. I'll probably just head to bed early."

"All right. Well, good night." He didn't kiss her again, although she hoped he would. Instead, he slammed her door, and then moved around to the driver's side where he slid behind the wheel.

He sat, watching her. She would have loved to think he was reluctant to leave her, but she realized he was waiting for her to get safely inside the house before he drove away. Zane might be the most frustrating man on earth, a paradox she couldn't figure out, but he was the type of guy to make sure a woman was safe before he left her in the dark, just as how he was the kind of man who'd chosen the best knife for her to carry to Nigeria.

He was also the type who kissed a woman breathless and left her alone and confused. With a sigh, she turned and made her way to the front door, digging for her key as she went.

One sleepless night spent pondering Zane and

this odd day definitely wouldn’t be long enough to figure out the mystery of the man, but it would be a start.

CHAPTER TEN

"Please, tell me there's some action on the horizon and I have to come in tonight."

If Jon said there was nothing, Zane was willing to beg the command to call him back for something. Anything. He'd even volunteer to do paperwork at this point.

Jon laughed. "The parents driving you crazy?"

"Um, yup." Zane wished it were just his father that was the problem.

Yes, he dreaded the inevitable conflict with his father as he drove at the actual speed limit—on purpose—just so he wouldn't reach his parents' house any sooner than he had to, but that wasn't the reason he was ready to hightail it back to base. He still felt the real reason seared into his lips after that ill-advised good night kiss.

Thank goodness they were both expected back at their parents' houses tonight. That had been the one thing to save him. The night might have ended differently if he'd been alone with Missy. If, God forbid, he'd had to walk her to the door of her own apartment where they would have been alone and unsupervised by the parental units, things could have gotten out of hand.

As it was he had to remind himself this was Missy. The girl who'd been like the annoying little sister he'd never had. The woman who his father was blackmailing him into dating—and into marrying, if Georgie had his way.

And dammit, Zane really did like her. If he'd stumbled across Missy at a party or in a bar, if she'd been a stranger he hadn't watched grow up, he'd have been all over her. Literally.

"Well, I'm sorry to disappoint you, but it's looking pretty quiet around here. Did you sign the contract yet?"

"No." Zane sighed.

Jon's question reminded him of the reason he needed to stick this out. One million reasons, to be exact. "I'm going to pin the old man down now and see if we can get that taken care of tomorrow."

"That would be good. I'm afraid to let myself celebrate. Not until I see it in black and white."

That was probably a smart thing, particularly in dealings with the infamous George Alexander. Zane didn't trust him as far as he could throw him.

"All right. I'll call you tomorrow. Bye." He drew in a breath and disconnected.

Maybe he should have spent the night somewhere with Missy, to make Georgie extra happy. Then again, knowing how warped his father could be when it came to getting what he wanted, next the man would be suggesting Zane get Missy pregnant so she'd have to marry him. As fucked up as it sounded, Zane wouldn't put it past his father to think that might be a good idea.

Shit. His father scared the hell out of him sometimes . . . and he was about to walk right into the snake's den and willingly spend the night.

The house loomed before him. Zane stopped the car and stared at the silhouette against the night sky. The rooms were dark except for two, one at each end of the house. His father's study and his mother's bedroom.

That's probably how she stood being married to him for so long—his mother kept a whole house in between them, not to mention them sleeping in separate bedrooms for as long as he could remember. That was, supposedly, because his father snored.

It was no wonder Zane had never had a serious relationship. What role models for a healthy long-term relationship did he have? Certainly not his parents. And if his father had his way, he'd push Zane into a loveless marriage of convenience simply to benefit his business dealings.

It didn't matter that Zane did have a good time with Missy today. He wasn't marrying anyone simply to please his father.

It wasn't lost on him what a hypocrite he was being. Zane was in fact dating her to please his father, which brought him back to the need to talk with Georgie. Zane had to cement the man's commitment to invest. Like Jon, Zane wanted that written down in black and white and signed on the dotted line.

To do that, he'd have to go inside.

He hit the button on the dash and the roof mechanism creaked and rose above him. He locked the roof in place and pulled the keys out of the ignition.

Grabbing his bags from the trunk, Zane headed for the door, wondering if his key would even work. Not that he needed a key. Most buildings he entered in his line of work he wasn't a key holder for.

That might be fun, actually. Picking the lock. Disabling the alarm, should it be set. Using every bit of stealth he'd honed for a decade to sneak up on the old man. It would prove to him how skilled Zane was.

It would also probably give Georgie a heart attack. Zane didn't feel as worried about that possibility as he probably should.

Flaunting his burglar skills might not be the best way for Zane to prove his worth and the value of his training to his father, anyway.

Amazingly, his old key still fit the front door lock. Wonders never ceased. Then again, what hadn't changed in his old home and with his parents far outweighed what had. As he turned the key in the lock, Zane knew from his earlier visit that the same table was right inside the front door, just as the same shrubs were still planted on either side of the front door, perfectly cropped so they'd barely grown over the years.

The small light fixture above the oil painting in the front foyer illuminated his entry. Zane set his bags on the floor. He laid his keys on the table. He didn't need to turn on the lights to navigate his way through the home he'd run through and played in for more than half his life. He walked the familiar path to his father's office.

The heavy wood paneled door was ajar. Silently, Zane pressed one palm to it and pushed. Standing in the shadows, he saw the older man's head bent as he read the stack of papers on his desk.

How lucky would it be if those were the papers for good old George's investment in GAPS? Zane hated to even hope. "Father."

Georgie startled at the sound of his name. "Jesus, Zane. Make some noise next time."

"I'll try." Admittedly, Zane felt a sense of satisfaction in seeing his father jump. He moved into the room and glanced at the papers on the desk. "That the contract for GAPS?"

His father lifted his brow. "No. I do have a few other things going on, you know."

Zane set his jaw. "I know. So do I, which is why I wanted to get this taken care of."

Georgie leaned back in his chair. "You and Missy looked cozy tonight at dinner."

Zane waited a beat to see if there was a point to his father's statement. When none seemed forthcoming, he said, "Isn't that what you wanted?"

"Not quite."

"You said to ask her out as a show of good faith. I've done that."

"You neglected to tell me she'd be away in Africa for the next three months."

"Because I didn't know. Just as I wasn't aware

of her father making a bid for the presidential nomination."

"Do you plan to secure your relationship before she leaves?" Georgie asked, ignoring the second half of Zane's prior statement.

"She leaves in a few days."

"And?"

"What do you propose I do in four days time after not having seen her in a decade?"

"That's your problem, not mine."

The reality of this situation was beginning to become clear and Zane didn't like it. "When will the contracts be ready?"

"I'm not sure. A week, maybe. Perhaps longer." Georgie shrugged.

His bastard of a father was going to hold the contracts until Zane had, as he'd put it, *secured the relationship*.

Anger rose fast and powerful within him. Georgie wanted to play God with the lives of those around him. He assumed he could because he had something Zane needed.

Fuck that. The cost was too high. The collateral damage too vast. It included Missy and Zane's own integrity. Not to mention getting Jon's hopes up while George strung them all along like puppets.

Pushing down his rising emotions, Zane channeled his anger into determination. He'd find a way, but it wouldn't be Georgie's. "Goodbye, Father."

"Goodnight." George went back to studying the papers on his desk.

Zane let out a short bitter laugh. "No, not

goodnight. I'm saying goodbye to Mother and then I'm heading back to base."

"You got recalled? I told you to take time off—"

"I haven't been recalled. I'm choosing to leave." Zane still had free choice. It was hard to remember that sometimes around a force such as his father.

A deep crease formed across Georgie's forehead. "How are you going to make progress with Missy if you're not here?"

"I'm not." Not as long as she was part of his father's bullshit conditions. She didn't deserve that. Zane turned and strode through the door.

"Zane." The sound of his father's voice followed him. "This little act of rebellion of yours is going to cost you a lot of money."

Doing what Georgie wanted carried a cost far greater than money. Zane kept climbing the staircase to the second floor and the bedrooms. He drew in a bracing breath and hid the anger that his father deserved but his mother did not.

Lifting a fist, he knocked on the door. "Mom?"

"Come in." When he pushed the door open, she smiled. "Hello, sweetie. How was your date?"

"Very nice, thank you." Zane moved to perch next to where she sat on the small loveseat, the book she'd been reading still open in her lap. He reached out and covered her hand with his. "I have to leave."

"So soon? You only just got here."

"I know. I'm sorry."

"It's all right. I understand how demanding your job is."

The job he'd likely be keeping since GAPS had

gone from viable to a pipedream thanks to his inability to buckle under to his father. Dammit, he'd let his friends down.

"Thank you. Anyway, I wanted to say goodbye before I left."

"Do you know when you'll be back again? For a longer visit next time, I hope."

He shook his head. "I'm not sure."

"I know you'll do your best. You always do."

What could he say to that? The truth was he hadn't done his best.

Tonight, he was a quitter. That he was giving up and walking away without a contract and without a million dollars was proof of that. But leading Missy on, using her for his purposes, would have been far worse.

Zane squeezed his mother's fingers. "I better go. It's getting late."

"I do wish you'd leave in the morning so you don't have to drive in the dark."

Little did his mother know that ninety-nine percent of his missions occurred in the dark. "It's all right. I've got Granddaddy's excellent eyesight."

"He would have been so proud of you."

Zane believed that was true. His maternal grandfather would have been proud of him for standing up for what he believed in, for taking a stand against Georgie in spite of the consequences.

Leaning forward, he pressed his lips to her warm cheek. "It'll be too late when I get home tonight to call, but I'll phone you in the morning and let you know I made it safely."

"Thank you, sweetheart."

Funny that he was in deadly situations daily—from missions to live fire exercises—yet he knew his mother worried most when he was doing something as simple as driving on the highway at night.

Zane said his final goodbye and ran down the stairs. Scooping up his keys and his bags, he headed out the front door and into the night without looking back. He didn't expect his father to come after him or try to stop him from leaving, and Zane was correct in his prediction. If Georgie had heard him coming down the stairs or closing the front door, he didn't do anything about it.

He tossed the bags in the trunk and put the roof down. He'd need the cold night air to clear his head.

Once he'd put some miles between him and his childhood home, not to mention his father's smothering presence, Zane's mind turned to the mess he'd managed to create in the past twelve hours, as well as all that had been affected. Jon. GAPS. Missy.

Pulling the car to a stop on the shoulder, Zane flipped on his hazard lights. He unhooked his safety belt and struggled to get his cell phone out of his pocket as he sat. He found Jon's number and hit to make the call.

Jon answered on the first ring. "Dude, there's still no action."

Zane wished that was the reason he was calling. He heard voices in the background. "Who's with you?"

"Rick and Chris are here."

Probably celebrating because Zane had made the

mistake of telling Jon he had the money before he actually had it. Crap. He had to tell them. "Where are you?"

"At my place. Why?"

Because he was about to crush their dreams on frigging speakerphone, that's why. He'd prefer if he didn't do it while they were at the bar or someplace else public. "Put me on speaker."

"All right." Zane heard the change in the call's sound even before Jon said, "You're on speaker."

"Hey, brother. I heard you had a productive trip," Rick said.

"Productive is right. A million freaking dollars worth of productive. You are the man." Chris's drawled compliment had Zane's spirits sinking even lower.

"There's something I have to tell you all."

"Listen up, guys. Let him talk." Jon obviously had guessed something was wrong.

If the other guys weren't so busy celebrating, likely with a few drinks, they might have heard the doom behind the tone of Zane's voice too.

"I'm pretty sure the deal's off." It was off if his father's parting words of warning were any indication.

The three were silent until Jon finally asked, "What happened?"

Zane's father had happened. "I honestly don't believe he ever intended to give us the money. I know him and how he operates. He would drag it out forever to get what he wanted out of me."

"But I thought what he wanted was you out of the military."

Snorting at Jon's question, Zane said, "Yes, well he's found something else he wants more."

"What's that?" Jon asked.

"Me, married to Senator Greenwood's daughter." Possibly soon to be President Greenwood.

"He seriously said that?" The shock was clear in Jon's voice.

"Yes."

"Now, I know you're a lady killer and all, but how did dear old dad think you were going to get this senator's daughter to marry you?" Chris asked.

"We grew up together. She always had a little crush on me. And as much as I wanted this thing to work out for all of us, I was going along with him. I actually took the girl out. I was willing to use her, a friend, to get the money for GAPS."

The guilt Zane felt over that was overwhelming, even though he had only let it go on for one day. When his father had started dragging his feet with the contract, Zane just knew the man would hold that money over his head forever.

Even if Georgie did, by some miracle, turn the million over to GAPS eventually, it would come with more strings than Zane could handle.

He ran one hand over his face. Pissed at himself. At his father. At the world.

"Zane, it's fine."

"No, it's not fine, Jon. I fucked up. I'm sorry. I blew this deal."

"Zane, we all know damn well you're always willing to take one for the team." Rick's voice came through Zane's phone.

"Hell, yeah. You stepped right in front of me and

took out that target who pulled a gun on me," Chris reminded them all.

Sad to say, but Zane was more willing to take a bullet than shit from his father. Maybe he should just go back and apologize, but there was still the confusing issue of Missy.

Zane sighed.

"Dude. Stop. We don't blame you."

He shook his head at Jon's words. His friends didn't have to blame him because he was pretty good at blaming himself. "I swear I was going to do it but I felt like an absolute piece of shit. She's a nice girl and she doesn't deserve to be used as a pawn in my father's fucked up game."

"I'm sorry she's involved, and I'm sorry I got you involved. We'll find the money some other way."

Zane wanted to believe what Jon said, but how they were going to do that, he had no clue. "All right. We'll figure it out when I get there."

"You on you're way back tonight?" Jon asked.

"Yeah. I just need to call Missy and hell, I don't know, apologize I guess."

"Apologize for sleeping with her because your father told you to? You sure you wanna do that?" Jon asked.

"No. I didn't sleep with her." Zane couldn't imagine how badly he would feel if he had.

"You? Didn't have sex with a girl?" There was shock in Rick's voice. "What's the matter? Was she ugly?"

"What? No. I'm not that much of a shallow dickhead."

Missy was beautiful and smart and sweet, and she didn't deserve to have his friends talking shit about her.

"Well, fuck me," Chris drawled out. "Zane Alexander *not* sleeping with a woman. You in love with this girl?"

"Shut the hell up. I'm not in love with her. I barely know her."

"I thought you said you grew up with her?" Jon asked.

"Yes, but that was years ago. I haven't seen her since I joined the Navy." Zane had already lost patience with this conversation, but he answered anyway.

The silence on the other end of the phone was very telling. Zane could imagine the looks flying between the guys. "Look, I gotta go and call her before it gets any later. It'll be late by the time I get back to base, so I'll call you tomorrow."

After a pause, Jon said, "All right. Talk to you tomorrow."

The line went dead as Jon must have disconnected the call.

Zane had let him down. He'd let them all down, and now he had to deal with disappointing Missy. She was the next one on his list. He needed to say something to her, but he didn't know what. He could lie and say he'd gotten called back to base, but deceiving her any more than he already had didn't sit well with him.

Things were too messed up already.

He checked the time. It wasn't much later than when he'd dropped Missy off since his visit home had been a record breaking short one.

Deciding it was still early enough she wouldn't be sleeping, he scrolled through his recent calls and hit Missy's cell phone number.

She answered on the third ring. "Hello?"

"Hey."

"Zane, hi."

"Um. . ." Zane was a fucking master when it came to the fairer sex, yet here he was stuttering trying to talk to a woman he'd known since childhood. Damn his father. He'd complicated what should be simple. Zane drew in a breath and got himself back on track. "Can I see you?"

"Of course. You said you'd call in the morning and we'd—"

"I mean tonight." Time for him to do what he wanted. What he'd wanted all day. Be honest with Missy.

"Oh. Okay. Sure."

"I'll be there in five minutes to pick you up. Then we'll go . . . somewhere."

"All right."

Zane disconnected the call and sat. He didn't want to talk to her at her parents' house, and he sure as hell wasn't bringing her to his. It was like he was eighteen again, looking for someplace private to take a girl. Sadly, the one place to take her where they could be alone was the same place he used to bring girls parking when he'd been home on summer break from prep school and college.

Great. He'd been fighting the temptation of the physical attraction between them all damn day. Parking alone with Missy in the same spot where he'd lost his damn virginity when he'd been a teen was the last thing he needed.

CHAPTER ELEVEN

Missy's parents were watching television in the study when she came down the stairs. She never wished she'd gotten around to moving out and getting her own place as much as she did now.

"I'm going out for a little while."

Her mother's brow wrinkled. "Now?"

"Yes."

"Where?"

"I don't really know. Zane's coming to pick me up."

"Zane?" Her father's gaze cut from the television to her for the first time since she'd entered the room.

"Yes. Is that a problem?" It was ridiculous she felt the need to ask that question at her age.

He shook his head. "No, not at all. You two have fun."

"Spending all day together, then dinner, and now going out again. You're seeing a lot of him." Her mother jumped on the bandwagon. It wasn't a surprise really. The Alexander's money would go a long way to help her father's campaign. Sometimes she really hated her life.

Missy shrugged at her mother's observation. "Between his schedule and my trip, we have to catch up when we can."

"Perhaps Zane is one more reason not to go."

She rolled her eyes at her mother's last ditch effort to stop this trip from happening. "Goodnight, Mother. Father."

Missy left the room before they had a chance to say anything else ridiculous. Waiting outside in the dark and the cold seemed preferable to being needled about her trip.

She didn't have to wait long. She'd only just closed the door and was about to pull on her gloves when she heard the roar of an engine.

Zane pulled the car to a stop in front of her and, leaving the motor running, got out. He walked around to where she stood. "Hey."

"Hi."

"Thanks for meeting me."

"Sure."

"You mind if we go for a drive?" he asked.

"A drive sounds nice."

He huffed out a short laugh. "Glad you think so."

She didn't understand his reaction, but let him open the door of the car for her before she slid inside.

Uncharacteristically silent, Zane slammed her door, walked around the car and got into the driver's seat. They drove for a bit without talking, him steering the convertible slowly down back roads as the cool night air blew through her hair.

Finally, he pulled off the main road and after about a hundred feet, slowed to a stop. He turned to her in the seat. “This okay? I didn’t know where else to go that we could be alone to talk.”

Talk? Again, he’d managed to surprise her. When he’d pulled up to the secluded spot and she’d seen the picturesque view of the river lit by moonlight in front of them, she’d assumed he wanted to be alone to do something other than talk. At least, she’d hoped that was the case.

“Yeah. This is fine.”

With a single nod, he reached for the keys and cut the engine. He unhooked his seat belt and then angled to face her. “I’m heading back to base tonight.”

“You get called back in?”

“No.” He reached out and took her hand in his.

“Oh. Problems with your father?” Missy took a guess.

“You could say that.”

“I’m sorry.”

“So am I. More than you know.” Staring down at their joined hands, Zane stroked his thumb over her palm.

“Zane.”

It took him a second to look up. “Hm?”

“I’ve known you a long time.”

“Yes, you have.”

“And I know when you’re not behaving like yourself.”

“Am I not behaving like myself?” he asked.

"No."

"In what way?"

"Well, for one thing, when have you ever in your life brought a girl here just to *talk*?"

He let out a laugh. "All right. I'll concede that point to you."

That victory she would gladly trade in exchange for a kiss. "What's going on? You wanted to talk. I'm here, ready and willing to listen. So talk."

Zane drew in a deep breath and blew it out. He brought his gaze up to meet hers and, lifting one hand, fingered her hair. "I'm afraid you're going to end up hating me."

The odd statement didn't do anything to slow her speeding pulse or lessen her desire for this man.

"I could never hate you." She raised her hand and laid it on his chest.

Zane lifted it to his mouth and pressed a kiss to her palm. "God, I hope that's true."

"It is. You have to know that by now." She tried to get closer, but the damn seatbelt kept her in place.

Blindly, she reached down and unhooked it. Once free from its confines, she leaned in, her face so near his she could hear every breath he took.

"Missy, we need to talk." He said they had to talk, but his eyes dropped down to focus on her lips as his breathing quickened.

"Later." She closed the distance between them until his mouth met hers.

Groaning, he palmed the back of her head and pulled her in tighter.

It was a real kiss, unlike the peck when he'd

dropped her off after dinner, and she was ready for it. Missy reached up with both hands to cup his face. She rose onto her knees in the seat, getting as close as she could. It wasn't easy given the limitations of the sports car's tight interior and the bucket seats, but she did her best.

She angled her head as Zane kissed her deeper. Missy couldn't help the sound of satisfaction that escaped her.

He pulled back just far enough to break the kiss. Cupping her face, he let out a breath that echoed her own feelings of frustration. Of lust unfulfilled. "We shouldn't be doing this."

Of course, he was right. The roof of the convertible was down and anyone driving up would see them. Besides that, the sports car was obviously not built with lovers in mind. It was pretty confining.

"Maybe we should go to a hotel?"

Zane shook his head. "No, we definitely should not, for many reasons. The biggest one being Senator Greenwood's single daughter can't be seen checking into a hotel with a man in the middle of the night."

"Then I guess we're going to have to do this right here."

He cocked one brow. "No."

"Why not?"

"For one, we're both getting a bit old to be having sex in a parked car."

"Desperate times call for desperate measures." And she certainly was that, desperate to have this man after what felt like a lifetime of wanting him.

He smiled. “I love how you’re so easy.”

Insulted, Missy frowned. “Thanks.” Her sarcasm was clear in her tone.

Zane shook his head. “Relax. I meant easygoing.”

“Because I’m willing to have sex with you in your car?” She shouldn’t be insulted, she supposed.

Missy was not only willing, she was more than ready. Hell, he could suggest they go pretty much anywhere and if the end result was her finally getting what she’d always wanted, that being Zane, she’d be happy to go.

“Because you’ll trade in your designer clothes and bags for cargo pants and military surplus to go to Africa for three months while all your friends are probably going to the Caribbean. Because when I called much too late tonight and suggested we go for a drive without any explanation, you came with me anyway without question. And yes, because if I lose my mind completely and start to think it might actually be a good idea to have sex with you, you’d be all right with that.”

She didn’t like how he was talking rather than kissing her.

Judging by that kiss, he wanted her as much as she wanted him, but it felt as if he was talking himself out of doing anything about it. She wasn’t about to let that happen. Not when she was this close to having what she’d imagined and dreamed of for years.

“Zane.”

“Yes.”

“Kiss me.”

He didn't, and that was her first indication there was definitely something wrong. He sighed and took her hand in his again. "We need to talk."

Normally, she'd be happy he wanted to talk since Zane could be a man of few words, always keeping things close to the vest. But in this situation, talking was not a good thing.

She nodded anyway. "All right."

Zane hesitated for so long, she began to fear whatever he had to say was really, really bad. Like I'm-sorry-I-kissed-you-since-I-have-a-wife-and-three-children kind of bad. Missy braced herself for the worst as he opened his mouth and drew in a breath.

"My father promised to invest a million dollars in the security company my teammates and I want to open, but only if I started dating you. I'm guessing your father's bid for the presidency was too much for dear old dad to resist."

As his confession spilled out in a tumble of words, she didn't know which was worse. That he'd asked her out originally because his father was paying him to. Or that even for a million dollars, Zane couldn't bring himself to continue doing it.

On top of that, she might just be the only female alive who Zane Alexander had taken parking and didn't have sex with. How humiliating was that?

"Oh." Missy bit her lip and pondered what to do. What to say. How to feel . . . besides sick to her stomach.

"Missy, listen to me. You have every right to hate me or at least be pretty damn angry. I called you because he wanted me to, but the more time I spent with you the more I liked you. That was the main reason why I walked away from this deal. I couldn't live with myself. I don't want to lie to you."

"Because you like me."

"Yes. A lot. Anyway, now you know. I'll take you home." Zane leaned back and turned to face forward in his seat.

"Wait. Before we go back, can I ask you something first?"

He rested one had on the steering wheel as he turned his head to look back at her. "Of course."

"Why did you kiss me just now if you weren't interested in me?"

Zane sent her a sideways glance and reached for the ignition. "I never said I wasn't interested."

Missy reached out and laid her hand over his, pulling it into her lap. "Zane. Don't take me home yet."

His eyes narrowed as his gaze moved over her face. "Why not?"

"This is why not." Missy tugged on his hand, pulling him closer. She reached up, grabbed his head and pressed her lips against his.

This time he didn't stop. He didn't pull away. He kissed her the way she'd always dreamed he would. He tangled his hands in her hair and angled his head, kissing her deeper, harder. His tongue stroking against hers set a rhythm that had her needing more of him. All of him.

"We should put the roof up," he said between kisses.

Frustrated that she couldn't get close enough to

him as it was, Missy shook her head. The roof above her would only make things worse. "No. We should get out and lie on the grass where there's more room."

Zane let out a laugh and ran his hands down her arms. "God, you're amazing. But it's winter."

"We're in the south. It's warm enough."

"Not for what I want, it's not." He drew in a breath and reached for the buttons of her coat, unfastening one at a time. When it was open, he slid his hands beneath the coat and ran his palms over her. "It nearly killed me seeing you wearing this dress all day."

She smiled. "You like it?"

"Yes." He moved to press his lips against her ear. "Of course, I'd like to see it off you too."

Missy couldn't agree more. She'd spent many a summer day waiting by the pool for Zane to take off his shirt just so she could get a glimpse of his lean muscled body as he cut through the water with a perfect dive off the high board. Now that she finally had her hands on him, he was fully dressed. But where could they go if he wouldn't take her to a hotel? Her head spun.

The answer hit her like a lightning bolt. "My boss."

"What about your boss? And shit, I don't even know what you do for a living." Scowling, Zane shook his head as he pulled back farther.

The last thing Missy wanted was for Zane to think he didn't know her well enough for them to be doing what she wanted them to do. "I'm the head of the fundraising department for the local children's hospital, and Zane, stop. So what if we didn't spend all day on small talk getting to know each other like a couple of strangers would have? We already know each other, and we were a little busy choosing underwear and weapons for my trip. Remember?"

He laughed. "Yes, I remember. So go on. What about your boss?"

"My boss Mina and her husband are away. I promised to keep an eye on their place and water the plants." When he didn't look like he was grasping her meaning, she added. "No one will be home for three more days and I have the key."

Zane's eyes widened. He dropped his hold on her hand and started the engine so fast she had to laugh.

He glanced at her. "You'd better buckle up. I don't intend to drive the speed limit."

Missy couldn't agree with his plan more.

CHAPTER TWELVE

Missy dug inside her purse looking for this key she'd promised Zane she had possession of.

Standing behind her, he wrapped his arms around her from the back and leaned over her shoulder. "Want help?"

"No. I know I've got it. I just have to find it."

"All right." It was all Zane could do to stop himself from grabbing the purse and dumping the contents on the floor to speed this process along.

Alternately, he could have picked the lock in less time than it took her to find the key. This bag of hers seemed to be a bottomless pit in spite of its deceivingly small size.

Finally, she emerged with the key in hand. "Got it."

"Good." He was moments away from taking matters into his own hands.

Now that he'd confessed his shortcomings to her

and, amazingly, she'd forgiven his part in his father's plan, he could give in to the attraction they both felt. The attraction he'd been fighting all day.

Zane was done fighting.

She turned the knob and pushed the door open. He waited just long enough for her to get the key out of the lock before he turned her to face him and hauled her against him while kicking the door closed with one foot at the same time.

Zane pushed her coat off her shoulders and down her arms. He tossed it onto the back of a chair and then his hands were back on her. He laid his palms on the spot where the curve of Missy's waist gave way to the swell of her hips.

The fabric of the rich blue dress was soft beneath his fingers, but he knew her skin would be even softer. He'd get to that part. Soon. Now, he needed to kiss her, so he did.

Raising his hands to her face, he took possession of her lips in a hard, deep kiss. He meant it to let her know this could lead to one thing and one thing only—him inside her.

She must have had the same idea. As he kissed her, stroking his tongue against hers, he felt her unbuttoning his shirt. She ran her hands over the bare skin of his chest and groaned.

Happy she liked what she felt, he grabbed her by the waist and lifted, carrying her across the room as she wrapped her legs around his back, all while they remained locked at the lips. He felt the spiked heels of her boots against his back.

Damn, that was hot. He'd be leaving her boots on for a little while after the dress came off.

They were in her boss's house. The bedroom was out of the question, as far as he was concerned, but not the wide leather sofa. He carried her there, dumping her onto the cushions and following her down.

The dress had a tie in the front that had tantalized him all day as he wondered what would happened if he should untie it. Like a ribbon on a gift, would pulling the tail cause the dress to open and reveal everything he wanted? Zane was about to find out. He tugged on the ends of the bow and pulled the sides of the wrap dress open.

He knew lingerie, and hers was some quality stuff. The intricate lace was delicate, the fabric high-end, but it was all just decoration. It was the woman beneath the bra and panties that was the most impressive. Missy was what attracted his attention most, not the underwear.

He ran his hands from the lace of her undergarments to the warm satin of her skin. "Christ, you're beautiful."

Missy shook her head. "My boobs are too small."

In the age of big fake boobs, particularly prevalent in military towns, Zane was a connoisseur of women's breasts, and Missy's were just the right size for him.

"The hell they are." Baffled by her misconception, Zane leaned low, intent on proving how wrong she was.

While he drew one of her nipples into his mouth, Missy tugged at his clothes. He smiled and grabbed her hands. Capturing them in his, he forced them above her head.

"Patience."

She blew out a breath. "Patience? Are you kidding me? Do you know how long I've waited for you, Zane Alexander?"

"I know. Sometimes I can be a little slow on the uptake." This was unfamiliar territory he was in, having sex with a woman who knew him well. One who he knew also.

This with Missy was different. She was a friend. They had a past. She understood him. He'd never been with a woman who knew him so well before—knew him right down to his childhood and family.

All that scared the hell out of him. He retreated to familiar territory. Sex.

She wanted his clothes off? He could do that. He stood and pulled his open shirt out from where it had been tucked into his pants.

"Bathroom?" he asked.

"Over there." She glanced toward one of the three doorways in the room.

"Wait right here." He strode to the bathroom as he undid his belt. Inside, he grabbed a towel and carried it back to her on the sofa.

"What's that for?" she asked.

"First of all, leather on bare skin—not such a great thing. Second, good sex can get messy." He was planning on having some very good sex.

She looked a little appalled at that. He'd distract her soon enough. Missy stood when he pulled her off the sofa so he could lay down the towel. Then, all his attention was on her as he stripped her bare of everything but the boots.

He hissed in a breath at the sight of her, even as she sat and bent down to take off the boots he was loving the look of.

"I kind of liked those on."

She shot him a look as she tugged one off. "I don't want to puncture my boss's leather sofa with these things. I'm thinking good, messy sex could also get . . . acrobatic."

After that comment, delivered with a gleam in her eye, the fact she'd known him forever, his faults and all, didn't feel so frightening anymore. Missy was funny and sexy, and she was stripping off the last thing she'd been wearing just for him.

Zane smiled. "I think you might be right about that."

She was naked and he was still dressed. He'd fallen far behind so he made short work of his shirt, tossing it on the floor. Kicking off his shoes while he unzipped his pants, Zane glanced up and saw the heat in Missy's eyes as she watched him. That was motivation enough for him to shove his pants and underwear down his legs in one swift move.

Removing his socks required he sit down on the sofa next to her, but that was convenient. It put him right where he wanted to be. Next to her. He turned and pushed her back, lowering himself on top of her.

He needed this.

There was a difference between wanting and needing. He knew that. Zane had spied women in the past, usually some hottie walking into a bar who he knew immediately he'd be taking home that night. But that was different. He needed this time with Missy.

Needed it as much to soothe him and make the pain of the disappointment he felt in himself go away, as to quench the ache inside him that she caused.

After quickly handling the necessary protection he always carried with him, Zane poised above Missy.

With the lights in the room all on he saw clearly every emotion written on her face as he pushed inside her. Their eyes remained locked until the feeling of being surrounded by her overwhelmed him and his lids drifted closed. He forced them open again. He wanted to watch Missy's face while he loved her.

Strange. He usually didn't care if he could see the woman beneath him or not. He'd usually close his eyes and just feel. This time, he wanted to see the pleasure in her expression as he stroked inside her.

He slipped one arm beneath her, changing the angle of his stroke, and she closed her eyes as her mouth fell open on a gasp.

A wrinkle creased the spot between her brows. He'd seen that expression on Missy before. Years ago when she was concentrating extra hard on perfecting her tennis serve. He smiled at the memory, but his goal was to make her stop thinking so hard. He wanted her to just feel.

"Melissa."

She opened her eyes, but her gaze remained narrowed when it met his. Reaching up and grabbing his head, she brought his mouth down to hers. She kissed him deeply, thrusting her tongue against his. The intensity of the moment increased until they were both gasping and he had to break the kiss just to breathe.

Her mouth against his ear as she gasped out his name had Zane's body tightening. He wanted to hold back but as her body gripped his tighter and she raked her nails down his back he knew there was no stopping it. There was no holding back the orgasm that barreled down on him like a freight train.

The climax seemed to shake him to his very soul. It drained him of all the bad that happened today. It emptied him of energy, as well, and he collapsed boneless on top of her. It was all he could do to catch his breath. There was no way he could have moved. He was content to just lie there and feel her heart pounding beneath him.

How could sex with Missy be hot as hell and yet so comforting at the same time?

Zane had clearly been missing out all these years, opting for sex with random women when he should have been looking for a nice comfortable friends-with-benefits situation.

How nice that would be to have a woman who wouldn't ask any questions. Wouldn't need any wooing. Who would just be there for him when he needed her after a tough day. After the night he'd had, it was damn nice to have Missy here to help him forget about everything.

"Tell me about this company you and your friends are starting."

His bliss came to a screeching halt at her

mention of GAPS. And that right there was why his friends-who-fuck idea wouldn't work. He wasn't in the mood to talk, especially not about that subject, but Missy was a friend so how could he be rude to her for asking?

He'd been content, drunk on post coital hormones and endorphins. He had been very happy to put his problems completely out of his head and let the steady sound of Missy's heartbeat beneath him lull him into a drowsy state. But she wanted to talk. She'd want to help him solve his problems, because that's what women did. The guys might give him shit on occasion, but they also knew when to leave him alone.

Grateful for the reminder of why he opted for anonymous sex even if it was more work, Zane had to deflect Missy's questioning. "No business talk. Tonight is for pleasure. So, I saw a nice big whirlpool tub in that bathroom. Let's go give it a try."

Her eyes opened wide as he stood and reached down to pull her up after him. "We can't do that."

"Why not? We just had sex on their sofa. How is taking a bath any worse?"

"I don't know. I guess it isn't." Still she looked too concerned to come with him willingly.

"I promise I'll clean up everything after we're done. Your boss will never know. Don't worry and come on. You know you want to." He dangled that temptation, betting she'd never experienced whirlpool sex.

Zane, on the other hand, knew very well all that a well-placed jet could do to a woman. He'd be happy to initiate Missy into the world of that particular pleasure. Buried deep inside her, he'd enjoy it right along with her.

CHAPTER THIRTEEN

Missy opened her eyes and tried to see the time on the bedside clock. It was later than she'd thought, but that wasn't a surprise really, considering. She stretched and the pull of sore muscles reminded her of the time she'd spent with Zane the night before.

The only thing that could have made the night better would have been if she'd woken with him next to her this morning. Maybe next time . . . which would hopefully be tonight.

They'd have to find somewhere they could spend the whole night together.

The fantasy of what that might be like played out in her mind. She imagined waking to the feel of Zane's hard body pressed against her.

Of course, she'd be late for anything she had planned for the morning were she to wake in a bed with Zane, but that was fine with her. Missy had begun her leave from work a week early to get ready for her trip so she had no schedule to keep.

The thought of leaving had her saddening for the first time since she'd planned the trip she'd been so excited about. That had been before Zane. Now, the three-month separation seemed like an eternity.

The memory of his goodbye kiss had her sighing. The subsequent memory of their time together in the bathtub jolted her into an even stronger reaction as desire coiled low in her belly.

He had done things with her, to her, she'd never dreamed of. And all in her boss's house . . . and bathtub. Missy felt her cheeks heat, but the shame didn't last long. Zane had cleaned up behind them. Her boss need never know.

The fact Mina was also a friend as well as her boss made Missy itch to call her, to interrupt her friend's vacation and tell her everything, like a schoolgirl. *That* Missy couldn't do. Not without revealing how she'd used her key for purposes other than watering the plants.

She wanted so badly to talk about Zane to someone, anyone, but even better would be talking *to* him. The solution to fulfilling that urge was simple. Missing him already, Missy reached for her phone.

He'd dropped her off after midnight. He'd kissed her, said goodnight, and waited for her to open the front door before speeding away into the dark.

At that time of night, it would have been crazy for him to drive all the way to Virginia Beach where his base was. He must have gone back to his parents' house to sleep.

That would be perfect. Then they could spend the day together . . . and hopefully the night.

His number was still in her incoming calls. As soon as she hung up with him, she'd have to remember to save his number to her contacts list. Just the thought had her smiling. She was obviously easily pleased, even with the most mundane things when they had to do with Zane.

She hit the button to make the call and waited for him to pick up.

He did after just a couple of rings. "Alexander here."

His very official-sounding greeting, delivered in a deep voice he must reserve for his Navy business, had her smiling. Just hearing his voice warmed her. She resisted the urge to giggle like a girl.

It didn't matter how young or old a person was, the first blush of a new relationship, when love was new and exciting and held boundless potential, was the best feeling in the world.

"Hi. It's Missy."

"Missy. I'm sorry. I didn't recognize the number."

"That's okay." This was all so new for both of them, he obviously hadn't saved her number to his phone yet either. "So how did you sleep?"

"For the few hours that I actually slept? Very well, thank you. You?" he asked.

"Fine. I just woke up. What are you doing right now?"

"Right now, I'm in a meeting."

That explained his very formal, official sounding tone of voice. "With your father?"

"No. I came home . . . I mean home at the base, not at my parents' house."

Missy frowned, not liking that answer. "Oh. I didn't think you'd want to drive so far last night. Or did you go back early this morning?"

"I drove back right after dropping you off. I'm pretty good at functioning on little to no sleep. That comes with the military."

She didn't know what to say in response, she was so thrown by the fact he'd left without telling her. Yes, he'd mentioned he was leaving when he'd picked her up before they drove to the river, but she'd assumed that after what happened between them, his plans would have changed.

"So what's up?" he asked. She had been silent for so long, he must have felt the need to prompt her.

"I just wanted to see what plans you had for the day. I leave in four days." She felt the need to remind him of that fact.

There wasn't very much time for them to spend together before she left. If he wanted to see her, it would have to be now, or at least during the next few days. Of course, maybe he didn't want to see her. That doubt had her feeling sick.

So did the overly long pause in the conversation before Zane spoke again. "Missy, you're going away for three months."

"Yes. I know."

"I've been through this kind of thing before. Between deploying and training, it seems as if I'm always leaving to go somewhere, sometimes for months at a time."

"Okay." What was he saying to her? That three months would fly by and she shouldn't worry?

"Chances are you're going to have spotty communications where you're going, if any at all." She opened her mouth to contradict him. To tell him that the school had told her that they had both a phone and internet, but he didn't give her a chance. "I really think it's better if we just agree to say goodbye now and not prolong it into a long drawn out thing."

Wow. No more beating around the bush. His words were like a sledgehammer to her skull. His feelings as clear as day. What they had had been a one night thing and now it was over.

"Oh." She was in such shock, Missy couldn't come up with any other response.

After another long, uncomfortable lull in the conversation where neither of them said a word, Zane said, "I'll talk to you when you get back. Call me when you're stateside again. We'll catch up."

Catch up meaning go back to just being friends? Or, in true Zane Alexander fashion, see if he's in the mood for a repeat of their one-night stand?

So that was what it felt like to be on the receiving end of one of Zane's booty calls. Missy now had the honor of joining the many other women in the not-so-elite group of Zane's past lovers. It sucked.

"Okay. Bye, Zane." A glutton for punishment, she hung on, waiting for him to say something. To take back all the hurt.

"Bye, Missy." He disconnected the call without another word as Missy sat with the phone in her hand, still reeling.

~ * ~

Zane put his cell down on Jon's kitchen table and glanced up at his friend. "Sorry about that. Okay, so back to options for possible financing."

Jon raised a brow. "Wait a minute. Give me a second to recover first."

"Recover from what?"

"That phone call. Damn, that was harsh. I've never been witness to this end of one of your relationships before."

Zane frowned, particularly annoyed at Jon's emphasis of the word relationship. His friend should know by now that Zane didn't do relationships. "What are you talking about?"

"I've been around to watch you sweet talk women right into your bed, but I've never been there for the big dramatic finish at the end. You know, the dumping afterward."

"I wasn't dumping her. There was no relationship to end."

"She know that?" Jon sent him a doubt filled look.

"Of course, she did." Zane answered Jon, but in reality, he wasn't so sure.

He'd never promised Missy anything, but women with far less of a personal connection to him than Missy, had in past assumed that one night together meant they were on the road to happily ever after.

Zane had made the assumption that he and Missy were on the same page, but he'd never spelled it out for her. Between her initiating their kiss in the car, and then her undressing him at her boss's house, there really hadn't been a good opportunity to discuss expectations or the future.

In his experience, those kind of discussions tended to be a mood killer. Bastard that he was, Zane usually didn't want to risk ruining what could be a hot night. It seemed easier to just clear things up the next day, if necessary.

That had always worked for him before, but none of those women had been a childhood friend. He sighed. Yes, he was a dickhead. Maybe Missy would realize that and be happy she'd dodged a bullet. She'd only be bound for heartbreak by trying to build something lasting with him.

Zane was incapable of being one half of a happy couple. With no experience, and no interest in getting any, what hope did he have of making a long-term relationship work?

None.

He glanced up at Jon. "Do you want to talk about my track record with women or about finding the money to get GAPS off the ground?"

"Can't we do both?" Jon's grin made Zane want to knock the cocky expression right off his face.

"Joke all you want, but we're both running out of time, you know. We've got to either turn in our separation papers or reenlist, and soon."

Getting out of the military without a firm plan of what to do next didn't sit well with Zane, but neither did re-upping, which would push their plans for GAPS out for years while they waited out the new contract.

The whole situation was starting to give Zane a

headache. "Fuck."

"Was that in reference to the company or the girl?"

Zane let out a frustrated breath at Jon's question. Truth be told, it was a little of both, but to fix the mess he'd created for the company, he'd have to forget about Missy. He pushed the guilt and memories away, put Missy out of his head, and grabbed the pad of paper and pen on the table.

"There's only one thing that's important. Funding GAPS. Is it after ten yet? I'm calling the firm that handles my trust fund. We need some expert advice on financing."

"Trust fund?" Jon's eyes popped wider.

"Don't look so excited. The principal is locked down tight. I can only draw on the interest, but I'm hoping by some miracle there's a loophole about borrowing against it."

Jon drew in a breath. "Dude, I really owe you for all you're doing."

"Shut up. We're equal partners. I'm doing it for me." Besides, Zane hadn't done anything yet except fuck up his father's investment and break an innocent girl's heart.

He reached for his phone to call his lawyer. Maybe he'd be able to fix one out of two problems he'd caused.

CHAPTER FOURTEEN

Missy drew in a swallow from the bottle of water. It had already been a long day and she wasn't done yet. It felt good to be able to take a break for the basic necessities, such as cold water and a trip to the bathroom.

"Thank you so much for helping me monitor the exam today." Diana, a volunteer from Great Britain, sat opposite Missy in the teachers' break room.

Missy waved her coworker's thanks away with the flick of one hand. "Of course. That's what I'm here for."

"No, it certainly is not. You came here to teach English, not proctor a physics exam for your desperate friend." Diana was about Missy's age and they had indeed formed a friendship over the past weeks.

Missy laughed. "As long as you don't need me to teach physics, we're good." Besides, it wasn't as if she was otherwise occupied. Certainly not with contacting Zane.

Nearly a month after the fact, that sore spot now caused more of a dull ache than the sharp pain it had immediately after that night . . . and that phone call.

"I was surprised so many girls missed the exam, though." Missy focused herself back on work, which was what she'd been doing since she'd arrived at the school in North Eastern Nigeria.

"Sadly, I'm not."

Missy frowned. "You're not?"

"No. There's a lot of unrest in this region. There has been for years, but recently it seems to be escalating. It's not surprising more and more parents are opting to pull their daughters out of school."

"Escalating how?"

"Abubakar Skekau, the leader of the Boko Haram, put a video on the internet a couple of days ago saying girls should not be in school. That they should be married instead . . . at age nine."

Missy couldn't believe her ears. "Nine? That's crazy."

"Believe me, I agree. Unfortunately, he has a legion of followers in the organization who believe he takes his orders directly from Allah, and they are willing to do whatever Shekau says, including killing and kidnapping. Fear of the Boko Haram is enough to frighten many people."

"What exactly is this Boko Haram?"

"They're an Islamic organization against the Westernization of the country."

"They sound like nut jobs to me."

"Well, they're jihadist nut jobs—as you say—who have the backing of Al Qaeda."

Though she hadn't heard of this Boko Haram before today, Missy had most definitely heard of Al Qaeda. No wonder Zane had acted so concerned about her coming to Nigeria. At least, he'd pretended he was concerned on the date he'd been required to go on with her in exchange for his father's deal.

That memory brought with it a good dose of anger, which helped with the hurt. Knowing the history and the issues between Zane and his father, and that he'd backed out of the deal rather than lie to her, she would have had no problem forgiving him had things worked out with them. But now, after he'd had sex with her and then given her the big heave ho on the phone, that initial deception seemed like just one more mark against Zane.

Missy had made the decision that day in her bedroom to put the mess with Zane behind her. Lesson learned, albeit one that took her a bit too long to grasp. The cutest boy at the country club did not grow up to be the best match for the starry-eyed young girl who followed him around like a puppy. She'd finally learned that lesson and learned it well. Zane was one scar she'd carry forever. Missy only hoped it would continue to fade with time.

As far as her decision to come to Nigeria, the reality was there were small groups of violent radical factions in every country, including the United States. Missy had volunteered to teach at a government secondary school located in a Christian village. It seemed unlikely the school or the village would even be on the radar of some Islamic terrorist organization. Besides, she'd been there almost a month and nothing more exciting than the ever changing weather had happened during that time.

Coming from winter in Virginia to Nigeria, where temperatures topped ninety degrees with eighty percent humidity and lots of thunderstorms, had been pretty eventful. Then there had also been Missy's first attempt at learning how to tend the beehives the school maintained. But even that had ended uneventfully, with not even a bee sting.

Diana glanced at her watch. "Ready to go back?"

"Yes." Not really. Proctoring an exam had to be one of the most boring jobs on earth, but it was time to get back to work.

The afternoon was rapidly ticking away and the students had yet to take the second half of the test. The one consolation was that Missy was sure the girls, all in their final year of schooling, were less anxious to get back to the testing room than she was.

Boredom. That was the main danger in Chibok, that and insanely frizzy hair from the humidity. Otherwise, Missy expected that would be all she had to worry about for the remainder of her stay.

CHAPTER FIFTEEN

It was already dark when Zane pulled into a spot and parked. Though to be fair it wasn't that late. It was just February, when the sun still set too damned early for his liking. But the days were lengthening with every passing square on the calendar.

All that did was remind him the time for him to either reenlist or get out was growing near, and they still had no financing for GAPS.

He was coming to the realization that their dream would remain just that. An unfulfilled dream.

Even if Zane did go back and groveled to his father, it wouldn't do any good. Not if the old man stuck to his original conditions for the loan. Zane wasn't going to take advantage of Missy like that, and wouldn't be able to anyway, even if he were willing to. After that phone call, which Jon had pointed out had been harsh, she probably hated him.

How he'd handled that situation was one of

Zane's biggest regrets. If he could turn back time . . . What would he do if he could do it all over again?

Negotiate a different deal with his father to begin with. And as for Missy, he would have never hurt her. He definitely would not have had sex with her, for both of their sakes.

The memory of that night still haunted him. He'd relived it more times than he could count. Even after all these weeks he could still remember every detail vividly. Memories kept him up nights while he was alone in his bed . . . and he had been alone. Zane didn't feel like going out and hooking up with a stranger or even one of his usual back-up girls.

It must be the winter blues. It was the only explanation.

That the team had seen no real action since the hijacking back in January wasn't helping. The good news was, by all indications that was about to change.

Zane walked into the meeting room to see Jon, Thom and Brody already there. He nodded a greeting to them and sat. "Anyone know what's up?"

"No clue." Jon shook his head.

Brody let out a snort. "Hell, I don't care what it is. Any action is better than no action at all, I always say."

Grant, the senior member of the team, entered the meeting room and stood at the head of the table. Zane hoped he had something good for them. Opening a folder he'd dropped onto the table, Grant glanced at the papers inside, and then up at them. "We have a TIP situation."

TIP. Trafficking in Persons. Of all the many horrors that Zane had witnessed in his time with the teams, human trafficking was one that turned his stomach most. Forcing innocents, usually children, into a life of labor, or the sex trade, or child soldiering, were sins that he hoped had many traffickers burning in hell.

Grant continued, “Twenty four students, all females aged sixteen-to-eighteen, and two teachers, one American and one British, both also females, were taken three days ago from a government secondary school in Chibok in Borno State, Nigeria. Boko Haram has claimed responsibility.”

If Grant was still talking, Zane didn’t hear. He was too occupied reviewing the details. Students and teachers were being taken right out of schools in Nigeria. He knew he should have convinced Missy to not go. He’d told her it was dangerous but he hadn’t stressed just how dangerous it could get.

Boko Haram was full of sick motherfuckers who thought nothing of killing women and children, as well as men and boys. They’d killed hundreds of students in just the past few years, as well as prevented thousands more from attending school through threats alone, and the Nigerian government seemed completely ineffective in stopping them.

Attacks were the worst in North Eastern Nigeria where Boko Haram had fortified camps in the refuge provided by the Sambisa Forest.

Shit, what region was Missy teaching in? Zane didn’t know. He hadn’t asked. He should have.

“The girls and teachers were reportedly loaded into trucks by the militants. Observation by locals in the region puts the possible location where the kidnapped girls are being held in the Konduga area of the forest, but I doubt they'll be there long. The girls will likely be sold."

Sold off to be wives or sex slaves. All for the bride price of just over ten bucks.

"Now here's the bad news." Grant paused and looked from man to man.

Zane's brows rose. If what he'd just heard was the good news, he was afraid to hear what Grant had to say next.

"One of the teachers is the daughter of Senator Greenwood." The roaring in Zane's ears was so loud he could barely hear Grant's words as he continued. "The assumption is that Boko Haram doesn't know who they have or they would have already made demands in exchange for her. Time is of the essence. It's crucial we get to this woman before they figure out who she is."

Zane felt Jon's hand on his back. "You okay?"

"Yeah." Meanwhile, Zane was far from okay.

Even if Boko Haram didn't realize who Missy was, the dangers, the horrendous possibilities, were still unimaginable. She was a blond-haired, blue-eyed, attractive twenty-five year old woman in the hands of human traffickers. She'd be considered a valuable commodity in the sex trade in too many parts of the world for him to even fathom, even without the added value of who her father was.

"The family has kept the abduction quiet. Only essential personnel know. But if it leaks . . ." Grant didn't have to finish the sentence. They all knew what would happen if the news got out. The demands would come, under the threat of her life.

Would the President go against policy and negotiate with terrorists, given who Missy was? This president had already done so once for the American soldier held hostage by the Taliban. Zane could only hope Missy would be as lucky.

"What's the plan?" Thom asked.

He was grateful to Thom for speaking up, since Zane wasn't sure he had the air in his lungs to ask the question.

"We're to prepare and hold."

"Hold?" Zane asked, a bit more loudly than was appropriate.

"Yup." Grant nodded.

"Hold where?"

"Here."

"Here?" Zane couldn't control the shock in his tone. "Why not there?"

Grant leveled his gaze on Zane. "Those are the orders."

"Why? You just said time is critical." Zane couldn't believe what he was hearing, or maybe he just didn't want to.

The military had a long history of taking the *hurry up and wait* approach when it came to action. He should be used to it by now, but putting Missy's life in greater danger by having them cooling their heels in the States rather than on location bordered on insanity.

"Apparently there's a British journalist trying to broker a deal. A trade. The girls and teachers in exchange for Boko Haram prisoners being held. The president wants to avoid boots on the ground if possible."

Zane fought to control his rising blood pressure.

"In the meantime, prepare your kits and stay close." Grant flipped closed the folder and picked it up.

The meeting was over yet the only action Zane could take was to pack. Sure, the items he packed would consist of breeching charges and state of the art weapons, but it still wasn't enough to soothe his restless need to move.

"Well, guess I'll get to it." Brody stood.

"Yup." Thom followed suit.

After Thom and Brody had both walked out of the door, Jon stood. When Zane stayed seated, Jon asked, "What's up with you?"

"It's Missy."

Jon frowned, so Zane elaborated. "Missy Greenwood. Senator Greenwood's daughter. The kidnapped teacher is the woman—"

"You grew up with. The one your father wanted you to date in exchange for the money." Jon finished Zane's sentence as his eyes widened with realization.

Zane continued, "And the woman you heard me dumping on the phone the morning after I slept with her." Only they hadn't actually slept. He hadn't even given her the courtesy of spending the whole night with her after they'd had sex.

"Jesus, Zane. I'm sorry, man."

Zane shook his head. "Dammit. I knew I should have tried to talk her out of going. Nigeria? A girl like her doesn't belong in a place like that. Fuck!"

Hindsight was twenty-twenty. Having such

clarity after the fact felt excruciatingly painful.

"Come on." Jon tipped his head toward the door. "The only thing we can do right now is be ready to go when the order comes."

"I know." Zane clenched his jaw.

This was exactly why they'd dreamed up GAPS. So they could make their own decisions. Use their skills to take action, without waiting for the politicians to finish their tap dancing.

If he'd done what his father had asked, if he'd built a relationship with Missy and had gotten the million dollars, they'd be able to go get her now. He could have turned in his separation papers already. He had enough time stored up, he could have put in for terminal leave for the last two months of his contract.

Rick and Chris were already ready to go, he and Jon could have worked it out somehow. They could all be on a plane to Nigeria right now, on the way to get Missy back. Zane and the team could walk into that forest encampment armed to the teeth and shoot until not one damn member of Boko Haram was left standing.

The way things stood now, all he could do was pack up his shit and wait.

His mind still spinning, Zane stood and followed Jon to the door. He wished he could call Missy's parents. Reiterate to them the importance of keeping this a secret. Tell them plans were being made. That he'd do anything and everything to bring Missy home alive. But it would be dancing on the edge of compromising operational security by contacting them.

A family he'd known since birth and he couldn't call them at what had to be the darkest hour of their lives.

Sometimes this life Zane lived could be really fucked up. If he made it through this hell and came out the other side, he was going to make some major changes across the board. He faced death too often to have regrets about how he'd lived.

CHAPTER SIXTEEN

The ropes binding Missy's wrists had long ago made her hands numb. That was probably a blessing since she was pretty sure she'd rubbed her skin raw trying to loosen them.

The tent she and Diana were being kept in was too dark to see much of anything. All she knew was that she was alive and that the girls were being held elsewhere.

The girls. She'd failed them. But what could any of them have done when the armed men rushed the school?

They'd all been herded at gunpoint into the trucks like cattle. The men had driven for some distance before finally stopping.

All Missy had seen as they were unloaded during a torrential rain was forest and more armed men. She and Diana had been thrown in one tent together. The girls were taken elsewhere. Missy hadn't seen them since.

She'd heard them though. Horrible, heartbreaking screams that made her want to scream herself to block out the sound. Diana had said if they were screaming, at least that meant that they were still alive. Missy didn't want to think about what was being done to them to elicit the bloodcurdling screams.

Bound and weak from days with no food and barely any water, there was nothing she could do to help anyway. So she listened, and prayed, and once in a while, when Diana was sleeping, she cried. And she vowed if the opportunity arose she'd get out of there, even if she died trying.

She didn't even have the knife Zane had chosen for her, never imagining she'd need to be armed for a physics exam. The men hadn't searched her. If she had the knife on her, in her pants pocket, she could cut her own ropes, free Diana and . . . then what?

Escape into the forest and look for help?

How far were they from anyone who wasn't part of this group who'd kidnapped them? She had no idea. It didn't matter anyway because she didn't have the knife. It was back at the school in her room. It had hurt to look at it, a reminder of their one perfect day that had turned out to be not so perfect after all, so she'd stuck it away in a pocket of the bag they'd shopped for together.

A girl's scream cut through the night. Missy pulled in her knees and dropped her head between them. She knew it would be the first of many screams that would last for what felt like hours, though time was a concept she was losing her grip of.

"We're going to get out of here."

At the sound of Diana's soft whisper, Missy lifted her head, wishing she shared Diana's confidence. "How?"

"I don't know, but we will."

The question remained would it be before or after the men turned their attention to her and Diana?

The screams continued. Missy dropped her head again and braced herself to endure them, embarrassed and ashamed that the sound bothered her when she knew the girl making it was going through unimaginable horrors.

The screams stopped abruptly, ominously cut off completely. The sudden silence had Missy lifting her head. "What happened?"

"I don't know."

A burst of machinegun fire had Missy's heart rate speeding. In the countless days since they'd been taken, this was the first time she'd heard gunfire. "What are they shooting at?"

"Hopefully, they're killing each other."

Missy understood what Diana meant. Dissent among the ranks might be a good thing. Then again, it could be very bad. Whoever had been in charge hadn't bothered with Missy and Diana. A shift in power might change that.

After the initial burst, there was no more sounds of machinegun fire. Missy barely breathed as she waited, straining to listen for anything that might give her a clue as to what was happening outside.

The tent flap lifted and she stifled a scream as

two shadowy figures pushed through, one after another. One broke off to the right, sweeping a large weapon in front of him, as the second broke off to the left, mirroring him exactly.

The men who'd taken them were loud and sloppy. These men were dressed identically and moved with stealth and precision. Their motions were coordinated and smooth, practiced, and for the first time in days, Missy let herself hope.

"Clear." One man hissed the words and turned to guard the doorway.

The second man came forward and kneeled in front of Missy and Diana. "Melissa Greenwood?"

The fact he had a distinctly American voice and knew her name had Missy's throat tightening as tears of relief clouded her eyes. "Yes."

He smiled beneath the grease paint smeared on his exposed skin. "Ms. Greenwood, my name is Jon and I know someone who's going to be very happy to see you."

In seconds, he'd whipped out a knife like one she'd seen in the case when she'd been shopping with Zane. He cut her hands and feet free, and then turned to do the same for Diana.

The moment the girl was free, she came to Missy's side and hugged her. "I told you."

"You did." Missy squeezed her back.

By the door, the other man spoke low. "Alpha team confirming we have the package plus one. Repeat, we have located the package."

His words struck her as odd. The whole night had gotten surreal. "Am I the package?"

With one hand beneath her arm, he lifted her into

a standing position. As he smiled, his teeth glowed white compared to the camouflage paint covering his face. “Yes, ma’am. You are.”

The tent flap opened again and a third figure pushed through. The man at the door swung his gun toward the man and then moved it to the side. “Good God almighty. Warn me when you’re fixin’ to come busting in.”

“Sorry, Brody.”

Missy recognized that voice. “Zane.”

His gaze shot to where she stood, wobbly, but alive and whole, and that was all that mattered. That and the fact Zane and two men who she instinctively trusted were here to save her.

Zane strode forward and gripped her by the shoulders. “Are you all right?”

“Yes.” Her throat so tight with emotion, Missy’s response came out as a choked whisper.

He stared at her for a few seconds, looking her up and down as if to assure himself she really was fine. “We’ll have the docs check you out when we get to Chad.”

The man who had cut her free, Jon, was busy turning things over inside the tent, even checking beneath the two blankets they’d been allowed as their only comfort. He turned. “There’s nothing we need to bring back.”

“We have to get out of here. There are so many men. They all have guns.” Missy did her best to picture the men she’d seen so she could estimate their number and warn Zane and his friends.

“Don’t worry about that.” Zane dropped his hold on her and turned to the other two men. “The minute Bravo team has the girls loaded into those three trucks we've liberated from our hosts, we're heading out."

"Have you found all the girls? There were twenty-four. Are they all right?" Diana asked.

Zane glanced at Diana. "We found twenty-four."

Missy noted he didn't answer Diana's second question if they were all right. A cold chill ran down her spine. She wished he would hold her again, even if it was just his hands on her arms and not the hug she needed.

The man Zane had called Brody touched his hand to his ear and then turned to Zane.

"They're ready." Brody headed out the door first, slowly, carefully. He popped his head back in. "Clear."

"Let's go." Zane hooked his hand beneath Missy's arm as Jon did the same to Diana.

Missy hadn't moved, or even stood in she didn't know how long. Her muscles were stiff and weak and she felt lightheaded as Zane half led, half carried her outside. They sped into the dark night toward a caravan of trucks lined up in the center of camp.

She tried to look around her as Zane dragged her toward the vehicle, his one hand on her, his other on the weapon slung around his shoulders by a strap. She couldn't believe they could just drive away. That the men who'd held them would allow that.

"Where are they? All the men?"

Zane boosted her into the back of the truck. "There weren't all that many."

Again he didn't answer her question directly.

He'd deflected her. She was beginning to see Zane could be a master at avoiding questions he didn't want to answer. She had to wonder how many times he'd done that to her during their one day together. If her brain wasn't spinning, she might have a hope of remembering their conversation better.

No matter what Zane said about the number of men, Missy wasn't convinced they were going to get away so easily.

Expecting to see someone come after them in pursuit, she glanced past Zane as he climbed into the back of the truck with her. Even as the trucks pulled out of camp, taking a path through the woods one behind the other as tree branches whipped past them, she waited for a shout or a burst of gunfire.

None came. Finally, after minutes and miles passed, she stopped watching behind them.

Of course, danger could lie in front of them as well. She turned her gaze to Zane, standing up and facing forward in the bed of the truck, his gun braced on the roof. He wore strange goggles attached to his helmet that flipped down to cover his eyes, a vest and a backpack. Not to mention a knife strapped to his leg, and a small gun on his hip in addition to the larger one he held.

Missy wouldn't have recognized him if she hadn't heard his voice, and after their initial conversation, he hadn't spoken a word to her. He was cool to the point of being cold. His motions were disciplined. His attention never wavered as he surveyed the night around them, watching for danger. Protecting them all.

This man she didn't know at all. Which was the

real Zane? The one she'd thought she knew or this one?

The man watching what was happening behind the truck while Zane watched what was in front, glanced quickly at her. "You doing a'ight, Miss Greenwood?"

She couldn't see him in the dark but she recognized the southern drawl. It was Brody who'd guarded the entrance to the tent while Jon had freed them.

"Yes."

Finally letting herself breathe as she squelched the fear that they'd be attacked, Missy looked around at who else was in the truck with her.

In the dark, huddled together and silent except for one who was weeping softly, were six of the girls. Diana sat opposite Missy, her arm around one of the students. Missy tried to catch her friend's eye, wanted to ask her without words if the girls were all right, but in the darkness it was too hard.

Maybe it was better if she didn't know. She dreaded seeing the girls in the daylight. Seeing what damage the men had inflicted.

"How did you find us?" Missy asked, raising her voice so Brody could hear. Talking seemed to help and Brody seemed willing to talk, even if Zane no longer was.

He angled his head to her even while watching the forest around them. "Leads from the locals. Drone surveillance. A damn good bit of luck."

That last part struck her as funny. Missy let out a laugh even as the tears started to flow. She covered her mouth with her hand to hold in the sobs. All that could have happened to her, all that had happened, it seemed to hit her all at once. Now that she might actually be safe, she couldn't hold it in any longer.

"Missy." The sound of Zane's voice brought her head up.

"I'm sorry." A sob followed her apology.

"Christ. Don't apologize." He reached down and pulled her by the arm. It would have been impossible to stand in the bouncing truck as it jolted along the rough road if he hadn't tucked her in between him and the back window of the cab. "Listen to me. I need to do my job to get you out of here safely."

"I know." Just the warmth of his hard body pressed against hers calmed her. She could handle this version of Zane if he continued to hold her like he was.

"But after we get back . . ." He let the sentence trail off as he looked down at her.

"After we get back?" She waited for him to finish.

At this close distance she felt him draw in a deep breath. Zane mumbled a low curse before he leaned down and delivered one hard, fast kiss to her lips before he broke away. He took one more look at her and then returned his attention to the forest surrounding them.

"Hey, now. I would have volunteered for that there duty if anybody had asked me."

"Shut up, Brody," Zane yelled to the back of the truck.

Missy saw Brody grin before he went back to watching the road behind them.

CHAPTER SEVENTEEN

A knock on the open door of the sunroom had Missy glancing up from her book. The warm afternoon sun had made her sleepy, but the man in the doorway had her pulse racing.

"Zane."

"Hi, how are you feeling?" He moved across the room and sat on the ottoman opposite the sofa where she'd stretched out.

"A million percent better." Especially now that he was here.

She'd barely seen him since the rescue. His team had whisked her and the girls to Chad where she was examined by doctors and interviewed by government officials. He had come to check on her before her father showed up and swooped her away. Zane had promised he'd see her when they were both home, but as the days passed she had begun to doubt his promise.

"That's good to hear." He covered her hand with his.

"Of course, my mother barely lets me do anything. I'm lucky she let me out of bed to come downstairs today."

He lifted one brow. "It has only been a few days since you've been home."

"I know."

"I'm sorry I couldn't get here sooner. Things move a little slower when you don't have the presidential fleet of aircraft to whisk you home." He grinned.

"There was room. You should have come with us—"

"I'm teasing you. We had some things we needed to take care of before we left. I actually just got back in the country today. I checked in at base and drove straight here."

That revelation erased all her prior doubts and had her falling for him all over again. "Thank you for coming."

"I wanted to see you." He squeezed her fingers. "So, if we can convince your mother to let you out, do you want to go do something? Take a drive? Go out to dinner?"

She wrinkled her nose. "I don't know."

"Are you not feeling up to it?"

How could she tell him it was because the last time they'd gone out it hadn't ended so well? Yes, they'd had a wonderful dinner, and even better sex, but that next morning—that had really sucked.

Even a night spent with Zane couldn't make up for the pain of having him brush her off the next day. She'd been through too much lately to be strong enough to handle that now. She'd survived Boko Haram, but she wasn't sure she could survive being dumped by Zane Alexander again.

"That's not it. I feel fine." She couldn't hold his gaze.

He reached out and lifted her head with one finger beneath her chin so she had to look at him. "Missy, what's wrong?"

Damn, she was as insecure as that thirteen year old with braces again. She forced herself to answer him honestly. "Us going out didn't work out so well last time."

"I know. That won't happen again. You have my word on it."

So that was how he was going to play it. They'd go back to being friends. Having dinner, but no sex, that way he wouldn't have to dump her on the phone the morning after.

"Oh."

Zane shook his head. "You have the most uncanny ability of imbuing a single word with so much. Would you like to explain that *oh*? I'm a man. We're a little slow when it comes to the art of understanding a woman."

She might as well be straight with him. What did she have to lose? "I'm not sure I can pretend it's all right that we're just friends after what happened between us that night at my boss's house. Having dinner with you as a friend, and then knowing you're going back to Virginia Beach or wherever you go to be with other women because you don't want to be with me that way, it hurts."

It felt surprisingly good to get that all off her chest.

"Missy, that's not what I want."

She met his gaze. "What do you want?"

He let out a short laugh. "Ironically, I want what I did everything I could to get away from before. I want you. Not just for a night. I want a real relationship with you. I want exactly what my father wanted me to do."

"Which you rebelled against. Just like you always did for as long as I've known you."

"Yes. I'm a fool."

"No. You're just being you." The rebellious bad boy she'd always loved.

"Can you forgive me?"

"For what?"

"For being a coward and for running away rather than get close to you."

Again, his running away was typical Zane. How could she fault him now for behaving like the same man she'd always known him to be?

"The moment you mentioned your father had suggested you call me I knew it was bound to be a problem. Zane, I've known you and your family for a very long time."

"Yes, you have." He smiled. "You might be the one person in the world who understands me."

"I might be." Missy liked that idea.

"Are you really willing to forgive me for all my many faults?"

"Yes."

"Why?"

"I guess I like living dangerously. Obviously. You had to come all the way to Africa to save me from my last adventure." She was joking, but he didn't laugh.

Instead, Zane leaned forward and brought his hand to her cheek. "I will always come and save you. No matter where you are."

"I know." She believed that. Seeing him and his teammates in action, it was impossible not to.

"And I will never willingly hurt you again." He leaned closer, hovering just shy of her mouth.

"See that you don't." She closed the final distance and brought her mouth to his.

He kissed her with an enthusiasm that matched her own, before he broke away. "Melissa."

His use of her full name brought her complete attention to him, even with as dazed as she felt from his kiss. "Yes."

"You need to know, I might be no good at this."

"Sex?" Missy knew that wasn't true. She had first hand experience as proof to the contrary.

He smiled. "No, everything else that comes along with it. Relationships. Love."

The L-word had her pulse quickening. "It's easy. It's just like being best friends, except you have sex too."

Zane laughed. "Actually, that sounds really good."

He'd just leaned in for another kiss, the first of what Missy hoped would be many, when she heard footsteps in the hallway. He leaned back again with a sigh as the unmistakable sound of high heels on a marble floor grew closer. They were both looking toward the doorway when her mother, followed by her father, came through.

"Zane." Missy's mother came forward, both hands extended and a smile on her face. "I'm so glad you're here."

Zane stood and took her mother's hands in his, accepting the kiss she delivered to both of his cheeks.

"Pleasure to see you too, Mrs. Greenwood." When her mother finally released him, Zane extended his hand to her father. "Senator."

Her father pumped Zane's hand. "Zane, we both want to extend our undying gratitude for what you did."

"It wasn't just me, sir. It was a joint effort. Every man on the operation deserves the credit."

"Zane, please don't be modest. When the negotiations that reporter was working on fell apart I thought—" Her mother's eyes filled with tears.

In an uncharacteristic show of affection, her father wrapped his arm around her mother. "It's okay, Martha. It's over."

Her mother nodded. "I know."

"Zane, if there's anything I can do for you—" When Zane opened his mouth, Missy's father held up his hand. "I mean it. You said you were thinking of leaving the Navy. I'm sure I can get you a position anywhere you want."

Zane shook his head. "I'm afraid that talk of getting out was a bit premature. It looks as if I have to stay in for a couple more years. The financing for the company I was looking to start fell through."

Missy knew exactly why the financing had fallen through. She stepped closer and laid her hand on Zane's arm. He covered her hand with his and squeezed.

"Really?" Her father asked. "Tell me about this company."

"Zane and his teammates were going to open a private security company." Missy took it upon herself to answer.

"How much start up capital do you need?"

Zane shook his head at her father's question. "It's a major investment."

"How much?" he repeated the question.

"I believe it was a million dollars." Again, Missy answered for Zane. If he wasn't going to do it for himself, someone had to.

Her father nodded. "Done."

"Excuse me?" Zane's eyes widened.

"Consider it done. I'll have my broker wire the money to your account in the morning."

Zane's mouth fell open. Missy stepped forward and took the opportunity to accept the generous offer since Zane seemed a little speechless. She stood on tiptoe and pressed a kiss to her father's cheek. "Thank you, Daddy."

"It's the least I can do."

"It will be an investment. We'll give you shares in the company. Or it can be a loan if you prefer, though I'm not sure when we'd be in a position to pay you back." Finally knocked out of his stupor, Zane stepped forward and extended his hand. Her father shook it with vigor.

"I'm really not worried about it, Zane. Whatever

you think is best. I trust you, son."

"Thank you, sir. That means a lot."

"So I hope this means we'll be seeing more of you around here." Missy's mother smiled.

"You definitely will." Zane shot Missy a glance, before reaching out and reeling her in by the hand. "I'll be around a lot more. So much, you might get sick of me."

The last, he spoke directly to her. Missy shook her head. "I'll never get sick of having you around."

Her father cleared his throat. "I think there's something I need to do in the office. Martha, will you join me?"

"Yes, I will. Zane, you'll stay for dinner?"

Zane looked to Missy. "Am I staying for dinner?"

She remembered their prior conversation regarding plans for dinner and her original noncommittal answer to him. A lot had changed in the few minutes since then. Missy leaned closer to Zane. "Yes. I'd like that."

"Good," her mother nodded. "Come, Peter. Let's give the kids some privacy."

Missy heard but didn't see her parents leave the room. She only had eyes for Zane.

The sound of footsteps were still fading in the hall when he reached up to cradle her face in his hands. "Not being able to spend the night with you, all night, even if it's just watching you sleep, is going to kill me."

"We'll figure something out. There's a really sturdy trellis right outside my window."

He laughed and leaned closer. "Don't tempt me.

And FYI, I really don't need a trellis to get into your bedroom window."

"I believe you. Just don't fall and break anything I might need later."

Zane moved in and hovered just a breath from her lips. "Don't worry. I'm pretty hard to break."

She believed that too, but she didn't get to say it as his lips covered hers. He kissed her until she realized just kissing was not going to be enough. She'd nearly died, and now she wanted to feel alive.

"Let's go upstairs to my room."

His eyes widened. "I'm thirty years old. I can't sneak upstairs and have sex with you in your bedroom while your parents are downstairs. Especially on the same day your father invested a million dollars in my company."

"Dinner's not until seven. We have hours and hours before they'll come looking for us."

He groaned. "Stop tempting me."

"Missy?" At the sound of her mother's voice, Zane took a step back and adjusted the front of his pants before her mother appeared in the doorway.

Missy smiled. "Yes, Mother?"

"We totally forgot that the Smiths invited us for a game of afternoon doubles. Do you want us to cancel?" Her mother paused in the doorway. "We'll happily stay home. We don't want to leave you. You only got home two days ago."

"No, don't cancel. Go. Zane's here with me. I won't be alone."

Her mother smiled "All right. We'll be back in plenty of time for dinner."

"Okay. See you later."

She felt the energy vibrating between them, though neither she or Zane moved a muscle until the front door closed. The sound sent him into action. He reached down and scooped her up into his arms.

"What are you doing?"

"Taking you to bed." He answered the question as he strode to the staircase.

"I'm too heavy for you to carry."

"Please, Missy, you insult me." His brow creased in a frown as he proved her wrong by sprinting up the stairs.

In the upstairs hallway, he finally let her stand on her own two feet so she could open the door to her room. "See?"

"I see. My mistake. I apologize."

"No problem. I'll let you make it up to me." He backed her into the room. "One word of warning."

"What's that?"

"I almost lost you and I'm still not over that. And I'm riding a wave of adrenaline like you wouldn't believe over that investment. I'm just saying things could get a little intense." The heat in his eyes told her he spoke the truth.

"I certainly hope they do. I expect nothing less." Missy grabbed his hand and turned toward the bed. "Oh and FYI? There's a tub with jets in my bathroom."

She glanced back in time to see Zane smile. "God, I love you."

Her heart swelled as she turned back to fully face him and said, "I love you too."

His eyes narrowed as his gaze met hers, before

he moved in for a kiss.

Missy knew this kiss was definitely going to be the first of many.

Thank you for reading!

If you enjoyed *Saved by a SEAL*, please consider leaving a review and look for Jon's story *Night with a SEAL*, Thom's story *SEALed at Midnight*, and Chris's story *Kissed by a SEAL*.

Sign up at catjohnson.net/news to receive new release and sale emails.

Kissed by a SEAL

Retired Navy SEAL Chris Cassidy knows the bro code—no messing around with teammates' sisters. However, Chris never was one for following rules. Besides, his teammate Rick's gorgeous sister Darci is worth breaking the rules for.

Darci Mann is tired of being alone. Since Zane, the bad boy SEAL she formerly had a crush on, fell in love with someone else and her best friend Ali found her own happy ending Darci's feeling her single status extra keenly. Though she suspects her brother's buddy Chris would be willing to change her status . . . if she decides to let him.

When a routine assignment turns deadly and Chris switches from charming joker to capable trained warrior willing to kill or die to save Darci's life, she might have to reevaluate her feelings about the perpetual bachelor and her own future.

ALSO BY CAT JOHNSON

Hot SEALs Series
Night with a SEAL
Saved by a SEAL
SEALed at Midnight
Kissed by a SEAL

Red, Hot & Blue Series
Trey
Jack
Jimmy
Red Blooded (print compilation)
BB Dalton (bonus read)
Jared
Cole
Bobby
Smalltown Heat (print compilation)
A Few Good Men
Model Soldier
A Prince Among Men
Bull
Matt
The Commander

USMC Military Romance Series
Crossing the Line
Cinderella Liberty

Oklahoma Nights Series
One Night with a Cowboy
Two Times as Hot
Three Weeks with a Bull Rider
Fish Out of Water (*He's the One* anthology)
Two for the Road (*In a Cowboy's Bed* anthology)

Midnight Cowboys
Midnight Ride
Midnight Wrangler
Midnight Heat

Studs in Spurs Series
Unridden
Bucked
Ride
Hooked
Flanked
Thrown
Champion
Spurred

Maverick Ranch Series
A Cowboy for Christmas
Valentine Cowboys

Texas Two-Step Series
Texas Two-Step
Cowboy Shuffle

The Trilogy Collection
Opposites Attract
Nice & Naughty
Just Desserts

Sex, Lies & Wedding Cake
New Orleans
Private Lies
Gillian's Island

Kindle Worlds
Game for Love: Game On

Bundles/Anthologies
Olympus
Cat Snips

Standalone Titles
The Ex Files
Beneath the Surface
The Naughty Billionaire's Virgin Fiancée
Rough Stock
Educating Ansley

Billionaire Bad Boys
Cat Haus ~ The Complete Story (Parts 1, 2, 3)
Before Cate ~ John's Story
Cat Haus (Part 1)
Cat Haus (Part 2)
Cat Haus (Part 3)

ABOUT THE AUTHOR

Cat Johnson is a *New York Times* bestseller and the author of the *USA Today* bestselling titles *Saved by a SEAL (Hot SEALs)* and *One Night with a Cowboy (Oklahoma Nights)*. She writes contemporary romance featuring sexy alpha heroes. Known for her unique marketing and research practices, she has sponsored pro bull riders, owns a collection of camouflage and western wear for book signings, and a fair number of her friends/book consultants wear combat or cowboy boots for a living. She writes both full length and shorter works and is contracted with publishers Kensington and Samhain.

For more visit **CatJohnson.net**
Join the mailing list at **catjohnson.net/news**